My Dear Henry

Henry

A Jekyll & Hyde Remix

THE
REMIXED CLASSICS
SERIES

My Dear Henry

A Jekyll & Hyde Remix

KALYNN BAYRON

FEIWEL AND FRIENDS

New York

A Feiwel and Friends Book
An imprint of Macmillan Publishing Group, LLC
120 Broadway, New York, NY 10271 • fiercereads.com

Our books may be purchased in bulk for promotional, educational, or business use. Please contact your local bookseller or the Macmillan Corporate and Premium Sales Department at (800) 221-7945 ext. 5442 or by email at MacmillanSpecialMarkets@macmillan.com.

Library of Congress Cataloging-in-Publication Data

Names: Bayron, Kalynn, author. | Stevenson, Robert Louis, 1850–1894. Strange case of Dr. Jekyll and Mr. Hyde.
Title: My dear Henry : a Jekyll & Hyde remix / Kalynn Bayron.
Description: First edition. | New York : Feiwel and Friends, 2023. | Series: Remixed classics ; v. 6 | Includes author's note. | Audience: Ages 13 and up. | Audience: Grades 10–12. |
Summary: "In this reimagination of Dr. Jekyll and Mr. Hyde, a teen boy tries to discover the reason behind his best friend's disappearance and the arrival of a mysterious and magnetic stranger"— Provided by publisher.
Identifiers: LCCN 2022020011 | ISBN 9781250833563 (hardcover)
Subjects: CYAC: Black people—England—Fiction. | Mind and body—Fiction. | Gay men—Fiction. | London (England)—History—19th century—Fiction. | Great Britain—History—Victoria, 1837–1901—Fiction. | LCGFT: Historical fiction. | Novels.
Classification: LCC PZ7.1.B386 My 2023 | DDC [Fic]—dc23
LC record available at https://lccn.loc.gov/2022020011

First edition, 2023
Book design by Samira Iravani
Feiwel and Friends logo designed by Filomena Tuosto
Printed in the United States of America

ISBN 978-1-250-83356-3 (hardcover)
1   3   5   7   9   10   8   6   4   2

*This story is for everyone who has ever wondered if
you are enough, just as you are.*

The answer is yes.

Before

CHAPTER 1

1883

WHEN MY FATHER FOUND MY GRANDMOTHER DEAD, HE LET OUT SUCH a cry that later our neighbor claimed to have heard it, even though his home was a full length of field from ours. I might have been convinced he was lying if I hadn't heard my father's wailing with my own ears. The sound of a man's heart shattering into a million pieces was like the cry of a wounded animal—fear and suffering all mingled together. A chorus of pain rising to the heavens.

I went to see what had happened and it was then that I saw her—my grandmother, my father's mother, her brown skin ashen and clinging to her bones like wet paper, her knotted hands balled into fists at her sides. The skin of her lips had curled back, exposing her teeth. Horrifying as those things were, they weren't even the worst part. The worst of it was the look in her eyes. They were wide open, staring up into nothingness. I don't claim to know much about the properties of one's soul, but whatever life had lived in her had fled, and all that was left was an empty shell.

I was told the corpses I would eventually see as part of my medical studies would not be wide-eyed with gaping mouths.

They would be people who had donated their bodies to the London School for Medical Studies, and their mouths and eyes would be sewn shut. My stomach lurched at the thought.

My father was the only reason I was pursuing medicine at all. He would see me become a doctor, though I might have been content to study law. My father didn't care about being content, but not because he didn't love me or because he didn't want me to be happy. He simply chose to take the path of least resistance.

He focused on respectability and impressed upon me the importance of how I must be perceived by the people around me. Those were things I could control if I made the "right" choices, though it never made much sense. I couldn't control how others viewed me, especially when they seemed hell-bent on ascribing to me any number of unfair or untrue attributes. My discontent was a weakness in my father's eyes. He had no answers for me when I asked him why, if becoming a doctor would grant me respect, nearly every single one of the handful of Black graduates of the London School for Medical Studies couldn't find a permanent position at any of the city's hospitals unless they were orderlies, body haulers, or groundskeepers. He knew as well as I did that I would have what I was allowed, and nothing more.

My mother was meant to accompany me to the city, but my father convinced her that I could manage the journey on my own. She and I both understood it was because he couldn't afford the extra train fare. I did everything I could to let her know that I would be all right without her, though I didn't really believe that at all.

The train lurched through the London streets under carob-colored clouds. Smoke in shades of charcoal billowed from chimneys, blotting out the sun, and people pressed in on each other as they crowded the streets. London had a great many faces, some of which were unknown or, at the very least, unseen by the average Londoner. To be poor was to be frowned upon, stepped on. To be poor and Black was akin to being invisible.

A pang of anger knotted in my gut. What I would give to not see those terrible, twisted faces looking past me as they trampled me underfoot.

I disembarked and made my way through London's bustling streets to the Laurie boardinghouse. My father had made arrangements for me to stay there during my studies, and as I came upon it in the early evening, after slogging through endless rivers of waste in the drizzling rain, it looked like something that should not exist. That it was still standing was a miracle considering the angle of the walls and the pitch of the roof. It was leaning on the building next to it, which was only slightly less dilapidated.

I knocked on the door and waited as heavy footsteps approached from the inside. A small viewing window slid open, and a pair of brown eyes stared out at me.

"What do you want?" the woman asked, her voice thick with suspicion.

"My name is Gabriel Utterson. My father—"

The woman slid the little opening shut before I could finish my sentence.

I stood there in the rain, clutching my bag and wondering if I'd somehow ended up at the wrong address.

The lock clicked and the door yawned open. The woman on the other side was small and round with a heavy brow. She must have used a footstool to peer out because she was a full head shorter than me.

"You going to stand in the rain? Or you going to come in?"

I quickly stepped inside and she slammed the door, locking it behind me.

"Leave it open long enough and someone is liable to run in here." She narrowed her eyes at me. "Your father told me all about you. Said you're a bit of a bleeding heart, and so I feel compelled to remind you that you are not in the countryside anymore, Mr. Utterson."

"No, ma'am, I'm not."

She nudged me into the narrow front room with a ceiling so low I could have reached it with my outstretched hand. It was warmed by a fire, its flames lapping at the damp bricks surrounding the hearth. There were chairs and wooden rockers all around and everything smelled of cooked meat and cigar smoke.

"Welcome to Laurie's," the woman croaked. "I'm Miss Laurie. This is my place. My rules. Got it?"

I nodded. "Yes, ma'am."

"You're on the second floor. Room seven. No company, no loud noises. You'll be out by noon on the last day you're paid up for and not a second later, or I'll have my brother toss you out. Meals are at eight, eleven, and seven. You're not here, you don't eat. Stay out my kitchen."

"Yes, ma'am." All I wanted to do was change my clothes and go to sleep. Only when she'd gone over the location of the outhouse and washroom, the laundry schedule, and the coal ration did she dismiss me and take up a seat directly in front of the blazing fireplace.

I dragged myself upstairs and found my room at the end of the hall. It was the size of a closet with a small fireplace and a sleeping mat stuffed haphazardly with hay, but the floor was freshly swept, and there was an oil lamp and set of clean folded linens waiting for me. The night was black outside the single window in the outer wall. I didn't even bother changing my damp clothes before I fell exhausted onto the mat.

I lay there for a moment, waiting for sleep to find me, when I heard footsteps in the hall. I waited in silence as my eyes adjusted to the dark.

The steps moved to my door.

I waited for whoever it was to knock, but there was nothing. After a moment, the steps retreated down the hall and I heard a door open and close.

Breakfast prepared by Miss Laurie was a soft-boiled egg and a piece of dry toast. I ate without complaint even as the hard bread shredded the insides of my cheeks. Other boys staying at the boardinghouse filed into the dining room and sat down at the large table in ones and twos. Most of them were young and they were all brown skinned. The dormitory for premedical students was on the school's campus, but it had a strict no Negro policy. Apparently, we were good enough to attend, but not good enough to live and eat with the white students.

As I sat lost in my own thoughts, a young man appeared in the doorway.

"Jekyll!" one of the other boys called out. The young man stepped into the dining room and as he looked toward his friend, his gaze met mine. He was tall, his shoulders slightly rounded forward. His hands were shoved deep in his pockets, and he hesitated, as if he was unsure about continuing forward.

There was a pull in the pit of my stomach. A flutter of nerves. Heat rose in my face and I quickly looked away. I took a breath and raised my head only to find that he was still gazing at me.

"Sit and eat," Miss Laurie ordered from her place at the head of the table.

The boy—Jekyll—sat, and Miss Laurie slid a plate of eggs and bread in front of him. I couldn't bring myself to raise my eyes again and look at him even though I wanted to. I was an entire train's journey from my father's home in the countryside, but I could still hear his voice in my head: *This is not something that will garner you any sort of respect.* His words were like knives—they cut, and the pain of them never left me.

I finished my food and put my plate in a wash bin before hurrying back upstairs to change.

Jekyll's face was burned into my mind. The rich brown color of his skin, just slightly ruddy at the planes of his high cheekbones. His dark eyes like ink. I shook myself out of my stupor and changed into one of three sets of clothing my mother had packed for me. Despite her best efforts, they were wrinkled and creased. I tried my best to press them flat. I laced my shoes, being careful not to pull them too tight. My mother had patched the soles for the sixth or seventh time right before I left home, and keeping them laced too tightly pulled at the already worn stitching. I put on a hat and went back downstairs.

As I reached for the front door, a hand clamped down on my shoulder.

"Where're you off to?" Miss Laurie asked.

"I've got to pick up some papers from the medical school and have them sent to my father, ma'am."

Her eyes moved over me. "First impressions are important." There was still an edge to her voice, but her eyes were softer than they'd been the night before. "Take your clothes off."

Confused, I clutched at my coat to keep it closed. "Ma'am?"

9

Miss Laurie raised her eyebrows and stuck out her neck. "Your clothes need pressing. What? You thought my responsibilities ended with meals and room assignments?"

"I—no, ma'am."

"Good." She held her hand out and I shrugged out of my jacket, passing it to her. I removed my shirt, and just as I was stepping out of my trousers—with Miss Laurie doing a piss-poor job of shielding me with a blanket—there was a flurry of footsteps on the rickety stairs. A group of boys came careening into the front room, laughing and talking among themselves. Jekyll trailed behind them and while the others seemed oblivious to my existence, his gaze found mine once again.

A rush of embarrassment crashed over me. I grabbed the blanket from Miss Laurie and wrapped it around my waist. But the commotion drew the attention of the other boys.

One of them cackled. "Sorry! Didn't know you were putting on a show!"

They fell all over themselves as they laughed until they were out of breath. Jekyll shoved them through the kitchen doorway, then opened a closet under the stairs as Miss Laurie disappeared down the hall with my clothes. I pressed myself into the wall, wishing I could disappear, too.

Jekyll found what he was looking for—an oversize wool coat. He walked up to me and draped it around my shoulders without a single word.

He couldn't be much older than me, but he was a little taller, a little wider at the shoulders. I avoided his gaze as he backed away and left through the front door. I pulled the coat in around me and sat in one of the hard wooden chairs by the fire. I didn't know what I was supposed to make of the gesture, but I knew it sparked something dizzying and exciting deep in the pit of my stomach.

A half hour later, Miss Laurie returned with my freshly pressed clothing. My shirt was starched so aggressively I was sure it would retain its shape long after I'd taken it off.

"I mended the collar," Miss Laurie said. "Is this the only one you've got?"

"No, ma'am. I have two others."

She looked thoughtful. "Somebody loves you. Most of the boys here don't have three shirts between them." She sighed. "Bring me your other clothes. I'll see to them and then you'll need to keep it up. People will believe in you if you have a nice set of trousers, a stiff collar, and good shoes. Keep up appearances because appearances lead to other things." After I redressed, she came close to me and adjusted my jacket. "Nothing is given. Not to us. Remember that."

"Yes, ma'am," I said.

"On your way."

I left Miss Laurie and headed into the dull gray daylight. The narrow street was crowded with people rushing off to work. The sounds of babies crying and carriage wheels rolling along the street filled the air. Thick plumes of black smoke rose from chimneys, blotting out the sky. I wove between people and horses and carts and made my way to Cavendish Square.

CHAPTER 2

HENRY

I SAT IN ONE OF THE EMPTY CLASSROOMS AS I WAS DIRECTED TO DO by the receptionist. There was an entire waiting room full of plush chairs and fine wood tables, but I was asked to wait in a classroom far down the main hall. Only the oil lamps in the front half of the room were on, casting the rear of the room in deep shadow. Long tables arranged in rows filled the room; I took a seat at the one nearest the front. There was a lingering scent in the air—sour, almost chemical. Something I couldn't quite place.

A few moments later, a short man with skin as pink as a naked mouse came in. He stared at me for several awkward moments before speaking.

"You must be Gabriel," he said enthusiastically. I stood up, and he reached out and took my hand in his sweaty palm. "I'm Sir Hannibal Hastings. I oversee this fine establishment." He narrowed his eyes at me and smiled. "You look quite like your father. Same strong chin." He released me from his grip and immediately took out a handkerchief to wipe his hands before tucking it away again.

"My father asked me to meet you," I said. "He said there was some paperwork I'm to retrieve for him regarding my enrollment."

The man nodded and patted his leather briefcase. "Indeed. But I am glad we'll have a chance to get to know one another before we get to the business of paperwork. Please have a seat."

He walked to the front of the room where a giant map was plastered on the wall. "I come from a long line of very distinguished men. Members of Parliament, war heroes. My father fought against Napoleon himself." He gave a long, heavy sigh and turned to me. "I must confess that when your father reached out to me, I was surprised. I hadn't heard from him in quite some time. His mother—your grandmother—was the head cook on my father's estate."

My heart ticked up. My father had never been very open about how he knew Sir Hastings, other than to say that he had a relationship to our family that stretched back several generations. The nature of that relationship suddenly became painfully clear.

"After 1833, everything changed," Sir Hastings said. "But I still saw your father quite often. Your grandmother stayed on with us for nearly ten years. She was an exceptional woman."

All I could see in my mind at that moment was the image of her sunken face and wide, lifeless eyes.

Sir Hastings cleared his throat. "All of this is to say that I feel some kind of affection for your father in the way one does for a beloved pet or a prized racehorse."

I bit my tongue to keep from saying anything. The taste of salty iron wetted my mouth.

He approached me with his hands clasped together in front of him. "I would have you here as a student so that you may find a station as a mortuary attendant or some such position to which you're most suited."

"My father wishes for me to practice medicine."

Sir Hastings laughed until his face turned an obscene shade of crimson. Little tears collected at the corners of his eyes and frothy white spittle gathered at the corners of his mouth. He wiped his face with his hand. "Under whose employ? Come now. Let us be realistic. Your—your nature is built for hauling bodies, perhaps even assisting at the autopsy table. We're always in need of good, strong men in that way." He readjusted his coat. "Of course, you will be allowed to attend and take the classes you feel are best, as long as you can keep up with the program, which is quite rigorous. But understand that when you leave here, you will only be able to seek employment at establishments that permit Negroes. I'm sorry to say that not a single one of them would ever consider you for a position of physician's apprentice."

The anger in my belly was hot as a raging inferno. It burned through my chest, made me light-headed.

"We are who we are, young Gabriel," Sir Hastings said. "There is no point in denying our true nature. I wish you all the best and I will of course keep my eye on you to ensure your enrollment does not cast any sort of blight on this fine institution." He slapped me hard on the back. "You'll be a shining star if you can make it through. A shining example of what your kind can aspire to if they simply had the will."

He reached into his briefcase and retrieved a stack of papers, sliding them onto the desk in front of me. Then he turned on his heel and left me alone in the empty classroom.

"Do you really want to be a doctor?" A voice cut through the cloud of anger that had descended on me. Twisting around in my seat, I saw the young man from the boardinghouse.

Jekyll.

Heat rose in my face. "I—I didn't see you. Have you been there the whole time?"

Jekyll stood and straightened out his jacket, but didn't look me in the eye. "Yes. I'm sorry. I didn't mean to embarrass you. I was sitting in the back here, taking a moment to myself. You came in and I—well, I can't blame you for not noticing me." He approached slowly. "Sir Hastings gives everyone the same speech. He thinks it's best for us to know our place. As if we would ever be permitted to forget."

He sank into the seat next to me. His skin was the color of the earth after a heavy rain, as were his eyes. The long lashes nearly touched the highest part of his cheek. His full mouth twisted into a soft smile. My heart nearly stopped.

"Henry Jekyll," he said. He stuck out his hand and I took it.

"Gabriel Utterson."

"Oh, I know." He withdrew his hand, but let it rest on the pale white oak of the table. His fingers were long and slender, darker at the knuckles, the palm pale. "There's always a lot of talk when Sir Hastings brings in another . . . student."

He and I exchanged glances. We had an understanding.

"Your father wants you to be a medical doctor?" Henry asked, his voice soft. "Does he understand how difficult it will be for you?"

"Of course," I said. "He was a medic in the war. He studied under James McCune Smith. But he wasn't allowed to practice anywhere in London, not in an official way. He started his own practice and served our community, but he always felt like he could have done more."

"More?" Henry asked as he stared down at the desktop. "You mean tending to white folks?"

He was right, but it still made me bristle. "It's not as simple as that. He found his purpose in caring for our people, but the white hospitals had better equipment, better materials. He wanted access to that, too. He imagined himself working in a place like that and treating his patients there. They wouldn't even allow him on the grounds when he went to inquire about a position."

"I understand," he said, glancing up at me with kind eyes. "My father is a doctor, too. A scientist. He works downstairs in the lab. Sir Hastings has been letting him teach, but won't allow him an official title, and his wages are barely enough to live off of. If it wasn't for my mother's inheritance, we'd have nothing."

"Your family is of means?" I asked, confused. "Why are you in the boardinghouse then?"

Henry shifted uncomfortably in his seat.

"I'm sorry," I said quickly. "I didn't mean to be so forward."

He waved it off with a tight smile. "Being at home is . . . difficult. And Laurie's is the only place within walking distance of the school that allows anyone other than white students to stay there." He sighed, and his warm breath blew against my neck. A ripple of excitement coursed through me. "My mother made arrangements for me there. I'd been upset with her. I wanted to stay home, but now . . ." He trailed off and from the corner of my eye I thought I saw him smile. He quickly pushed his chair back and stood up. "Your father wants you to follow in his footsteps, knowing that he himself had to endure such unfairness . . . but what do *you* want to do, Gabriel? Something tells me this is not a path you would have chosen for yourself."

"It's not," I said. "I want to study law."

Henry grinned and slid his hands into the pockets of his jacket. "A lawyer?" He looked me over from head to toe. "That suits you." He walked to the door, then turned back to me. "I'll see you in class then?"

I nodded and he disappeared, leaving me alone with my racing thoughts.

CHAPTER 3

Dr. Jekyll Sr.

My first weeks at the London School for Medical Studies were filled with anatomy lessons, chemical studies, and memorizing the various uses of pharmaceuticals. Henry and I sat in the back of our classes and lectures taking notes. Henry took in every detail. His pursuit of knowledge was insatiable, and his quiet manner left me utterly taken with him.

Henry was a far better pupil than I had ever been, and nowhere was this more apparent than when we sat in the dimly lit former operating theater. Tucked away in the basement of the school, the makeshift classroom was shadowy, and the sour chemical smell was more pungent there than anywhere else. Henry informed me that what I'd been smelling was in fact formaldehyde, and that somewhere in the bowels of the school was the room where the corpses were kept.

Dr. Jekyll was a tall man with broad shoulders and a neatly trimmed beard of black scattered with errant gray strands. He peered through his round spectacles as we took our seats. Henry preferred to sit at the rail in the seats closest to his father. It was the only class in which we were permitted to do so.

"We will pick up where we left off," Dr. Jekyll began. His voice was hoarse, and as he laid out our instruction plan for the two hours we'd spend with him, he lost his train of thought several times and had to start his sentences over again.

"Is your father all right?" I asked in a whisper.

Henry gave me a quick nod. "He had a very late night. He's been working constantly in his lab."

"He has his own laboratory?" I asked.

"Yes, and he spends so much time there I barely see him when I'm home. It's almost an obsession."

"Obsession with what?"

Henry opened his mouth to speak, but his father cleared his throat loudly. "Am I interrupting you, Henry?" he asked. "Perhaps you'd like to teach this class?"

I sank down in my seat.

"No, sir," said Henry. He shuffled his notes and lowered his gaze.

"No?" Dr. Jekyll asked. "Then I would have your attention and your silence."

Henry nodded and I gently pressed my shoulder against his. I hadn't had many interactions with Dr. Jekyll outside of class. I had seen him in the halls, or taking his lunch in the courtyard. He seemed a highly intelligent man who preferred the company of his notes and books to other people. Clearly there was some issue between father and son, but my friendship with Henry felt too new to press the subject. My shoulder against his was my way of telling him he could lean on me if he needed to.

"Let us proceed." Dr. Jekyll moved to the blackboard mounted on a rolling scaffolding and produced a piece of chalk. "We speak often of formulation and chemical compounds. The language we use is quite clinical, as it should be for a learning environment such as this, but let us not forget that all of this is in the pursuit of the betterment of mankind. To cure what ails. To mend a broken body. To heal a wound—"

"The physical body," Henry said, loudly enough for me and others sitting nearby to hear.

Dr. Jekyll turned to his son. So did I. It was unusual for Henry to speak out of turn, but this objection had burst from him like water from a punctured dam.

"Is the study of the mind what you wish to explore?" Dr. Jekyll asked.

I expected anger for the interruption, but instead there was a curious quality to Dr. Jekyll's tone. He almost seemed surprised.

"Don't we need to do both?" Henry asked. "Study the mind and the body together as one? We cannot separate the two."

"The mind and the body?" Dr. Jekyll and his son stared intently at each other. "Of course the two are intertwined. But think on this, Henry: If they are tied together, it is quite possible that they can also be untied. And what then?"

A murmur radiated through the audience, hushed voices and

stifled laughter. I didn't know enough to have an opinion, but clearly Dr. Jekyll and his son shared the same fervor for the science of it all. Henry was gripping his pen so tightly the veins on the back of his hand rose to the surface.

What I noticed in that moment was how similar their personalities and temperaments were. They both possessed a keen intellect, but kept to themselves. The most striking difference was that while Henry was gentle, his father seemed angry under his quietude.

Dr. Jekyll moved on from Henry's questioning without another word on the matter. He spoke of his experimentations with chemical compounds that induced sleep, delirium, and even euphoria. He'd concocted a number of different serums that he displayed proudly in an assortment of oddly shaped bottles and flasks. On his blackboard he jotted down the individual formularies and took questions from the other students.

Dr. Jekyll set down his chalk just as the operating theater door swung open. Sir Hastings swept in without any regard to the lesson, his face a twisted mask of anger.

I glanced at Henry, who looked on with concern in his eyes.

"You'll excuse my interruption," Sir Hastings said.

"Will I?" Dr. Jekyll asked, and he purposely turned his back to Sir Hastings.

A grin spread across Henry's face and he leaned in close to me. "My father hates Sir Hastings as much as we do, only he's not afraid to show it."

"I feel like he should be," I whispered.

My father was always impressing upon me the importance of politeness, of professional courtesy. He said it would take me further than my grades or even my skills, though I did not think politeness would save me from the wrath of someone like Sir Hastings should I ever run afoul of him.

Sir Hastings straightened up and cleared his throat, glaring at the back of Dr. Jekyll's head, who still refused to turn and face him.

"A shipment of laboratory supplies for the upperclassmen arrived this morning, and it seems that it has now been misplaced." Sir Hastings tapped his foot against the uneven stone floor, and the sound echoed through the operating theater like a metronome.

Dr. Jekyll angled his head as he scribbled another formula on the blackboard. "I assume there's a reason you're telling me this, but I have yet to pin down exactly what that reason is."

Sir Hastings's face turned a shade of red I'd never seen in nature. He glanced around and I wanted to say to him *Yes, we had all heard Dr. Jekyll say that to you*, but I kept quiet.

"I would remind you to watch your tone and to remember your place." Sir Hastings surveyed the room and his gaze landed on Henry. "Set a better example for your son lest he think you a brute."

Dr. Jekyll stopped writing mid-equation. The tip of the chalk pressed into the board until bits of it flaked off and floated to the floor below. He glanced over his shoulder, then back to Sir Hastings. "What is so pressing? Can't you ask a student to track down the shipment? It can't have disappeared all on its own."

"You signed for it," Sir Hastings said. "Your signature is on the log. What did you do with it after it came into your possession?"

"I placed it in the supply room." Dr. Jekyll continued to scribble out his formulas on the blackboard. "Every faculty member on this campus has access to that room." He turned to Sir Hastings, giving him his full attention for the first time. "You've questioned me thoroughly and I've given you my answer. I am certain your questioning of the other two hundred and twenty-eight members of staff will be equally robust." Then he pivoted and faced the students. "Please copy the formulation I've prepared and tell me what method would be best for distillation, and how many cycles of distillations would be needed to obtain a pure compound."

I quickly began to copy the formula into my notes as Sir Hastings stood stunned for several seconds before rushing out of the room in a flurry of angry huffs and profuse sweating.

Dr. Jekyll let out a long, exasperated sigh.

———

After class, Henry and I meandered out as the other students hurried from the dank basement room. Lanyon, a young man I'd met on a few separate occasions, brushed by me and gave me a wave as he left. I prepared to follow him but Henry hung back.

"They should give your father another room to teach in," I said, covering my nose and mouth with the flap of my jacket. "The smell is nauseating."

"And let him think he's on the same level as the other faculty?" Henry asked sarcastically. "Hastings would never allow it."

In the classroom behind us, Dr. Jekyll went into his cramped office at the back of the theater. There was a loud metallic noise, like a rusted hinge being pried open, followed by an eerie quiet.

"What in the world was that?" I asked.

"He's going to the sub-basement," Henry said quietly.

I looked down at the stone floor and wondered what could possibly lurk beneath. The sub-basement was home to the morgue, and on more than one occasion I'd heard rumors of terrible cries echoing up from the lower level through the vents.

"Why is your father going down there?" I asked.

Henry put his hands in his pockets and shook his head. "That's where they keep the bodies."

"Your father is a chemist. What would he need with a corpse?"

Henry shrugged. "I don't know. He never speaks of it. But that noise was the sound of the chute opening and closing." Henry gestured toward the former operating theater. "Anatomical dissections used to be performed in there and they needed a way to get the bodies down to the morgue to be disposed of afterward."

"And your father uses that to get down there?" I was horrified at the thought.

"Do you want to see it?" Henry asked.

I whipped my head around. "You can't be serious."

But Henry was already walking toward Dr. Jekyll's office. "I've always wanted to know what goes on down there, but students aren't allowed without a faculty chaperone."

I caught up with him and grabbed hold of his sleeve. "Henry, no. We can't."

Henry turned to me; I'd expected to see a mischievous grin stretched across his face, but I saw only a pained expression.

"My father is a very secretive man," Henry said, his voice low and trembling. "I enjoy my studies here for the most part, and I want so much to share that with him. If he would just let me in on whatever it is he's working on, maybe I could assist him."

Henry and I were so much alike—we both wanted very much to please our fathers, to find common ground. Up to that point I had been drawn to Henry for a great number of reasons—his eyes, his smile, his quiet manner. But there was so much more to him than those outward things. I wanted to know everything there was to know about him, including his delicate, complicated feelings toward his father. I hoped he would confide in me all of his fears, all of his hopes.

I gently squeezed his arm and sighed. "I'm with you," I said. "But I feel that I should let you know that I'm terrified of the dark."

Henry chuckled. "It is not the dark you fear, but the things that lurk there."

"That's not helping at all," I said.

Henry's face lit up and he grabbed my hand, pulling me toward his father's office. He peered through the small rectangular window in the door, then pushed it open.

The space was clearly meant to be some kind of storage closet. The walls were so close I could almost touch them at the same time with my outstretched arms. A mismatched collection of bookshelves stood against one wall and a small desk scattered with textbooks and stacks of paper sat in the middle. Henry rounded the desk and stood in front of a rusted metal door, which was partially obscured by a hanging tapestry and no taller than his shoulder.

He grasped the handle and pulled. The door groaned and we both stopped breathing. I glanced back through the office door, toward the operating theater. No one was there; I imagined that if anyone had heard the noise, they weren't rushing to investigate.

I wondered if they would come even if they heard the sound of my screams.

A gust of fetid air wafted out of the narrow passageway behind the door. I cupped my hand over my nose and Henry reared back.

"This is a mistake," I said, doubt taking complete control of me. "Come, Henry."

I tried to steer him away from the door, but he planted his feet and refused to budge. I could see in his face that he knew this was a terrible idea, and still he wanted to push on. I sighed and took a small oil lamp from Dr. Jekyll's desk and struck a match to light it.

"At least we'll be able to see where we're going," I said.

Henry smiled, and we entered the narrow opening single file.

The slope of the chute was so steep that I could have slid down. As it was, every foot or so, a large chunk of the flat surface had been cut into a makeshift step. The little indentations were the only thing keeping me and Henry from tumbling to our deaths.

I gripped Henry's coat as we descended into the inky blackness below. The putrid smell grew stronger, and the temperature plummeted with each footstep. The oil lamp illuminated the cramped space, revealing a long-abandoned length of frayed rope looped through rusted pulleys.

"The bodies would go on a sled, and they would winch them up when they needed them," Henry whispered. "When they sent them back down they didn't use the rope at all. They just let them fall straight to the bottom."

"I don't want to talk about that while we're in here," I said, pressing my hand to Henry's back, hoping to prod him along a little faster.

We finally reached a small platform where the chute terminated and I all but fell out of the passageway behind Henry. I leaned forward and tried to catch my breath.

"Easy, Gabriel," Henry said. He looked me over. "You're not hurt, are you?"

"No," I said. I was, however, as frightened as I'd ever been.

As I stood and took in our new surroundings, I was shocked into silence. Rounded archways led to a series of tunnels lit by flickering torches. The ceiling was low and gave the impression of being far under the ground, like a catacomb. The horrid smell was overwhelming; I didn't dare open my mouth to speak for fear I would be sick. Henry glanced at me as if to ask *Which way?* and I shrugged. How was I to know?

Henry veered right and we moved down the tunnel in silence, keeping ourselves pressed against the stone wall. There was a din of voices, but I could not tell if it was above me or somewhere ahead. I imagined the unintelligible whispers coming from the mouths of the dead, and a shudder rippled through me.

Rooms branched off the tunnel to my left and right. Some had doors, others did not. Some were filled with old desks and chairs all piled up, and others held laboratory equipment. In a dark room lit by a single torch, a dozen steel tables sat side by side. Bodies draped in crisp white sheets lay across them. My heart beat against my ribs as I spotted a pair of bare feet protruding from under one of the sheets; a paper tag with writing scrawled across it hung from the big toe. I steadied myself against the damp wall as Henry stared unblinking into the room.

Just as I was preparing to suggest that we turn back immediately, Henry took a cautious step toward a set of heavy double doors. One side sat slightly ajar and I caught a glimpse of Dr. Jekyll in the dimly lit space beyond. He was standing at a table, another man opposite him.

"Did you do as I instructed?" Dr. Jekyll asked. "You followed the procedure exactly as I told you?"

"Yes," the other man said. He produced a needle the length of my middle finger and drew a length of waxy thread through its eye. "The results were . . . unexpected."

Dr. Jekyll stepped to the side, and it was only then that I saw a man lying on his back on the table in front of him. Naked and stiff, the corpse's chest cavity was splayed open. Vomit rose in the back of my throat, and a wave of dizziness threatened to knock me off my feet. I crouched and pressed myself against the wall, shutting my eyes.

"Did you record the findings?" asked Dr. Jekyll.

I opened my eyes just as the other man pierced a flap of skin with the needle and began to suture the corpse's chest closed. "You told me not to write any of it down."

"Good man," Dr. Jekyll said.

"The compound was administered and right away there was a distinct change in the appearance of the body," the man said as he continued stitching. With each new pass through the stiff skin of the corpse's chest there came a terrible sound like fingernails creasing a sheet of paper; it set my teeth on edge. "He was changed. But I wonder if any of this even matters? Experimenting on dead tissue is one thing—the process in a living body could be completely different."

"Let me worry about that," Dr. Jekyll grumbled.

"Come with me," the man said as he stuck his needle into the corpse's chest and wiped his hands on his smock. "I'll show you what I've found and you can do with the information as you see fit. Any chance you'll let me in on your little secret?"

Dr. Jekyll scoffed. "None. And if you whisper a word of this to anyone, I'll have you put out."

The man spun around. "Don't you go threatening me, Jekyll. We're both on thin ice with Hastings. You're not better than me just because you spend most of your time above ground. If it were up to Hastings he'd have you down here with me sewing up corpses like Christmas hams."

The man turned on his heel and led Dr. Jekyll into an adjoining room. I immediately stood and turned to leave, but Henry lingered at the door and then entered the room where the naked corpse lay.

I rushed in after him, and as hard as I tried I could not avoid the horror that lay before me.

The pallor of the man's skin was sickly gray and his chest had been sliced open and emptied, the organs removed. His eyes were wide open. They were not empty and hollow like my grandmother's had been—they were full of rot, and the room smelled of decomposing flesh and the fluid that tried desperately to keep the decay from spreading.

"Henry," I gasped as the smell hit the back of my throat. "Henry, please . . . We have to go—"

"Look at him," Henry said as he raised his gaze to meet mine. "My father is experimenting on dead bodies? I—I don't understand."

"Neither do I, but we can figure it out after we leave this place." Sweat slicked my back and forehead, my heart beating wildly in my chest.

Henry suddenly seemed to sober and he rounded the table, leaving the corpse to its fate. We raced to the chute and shimmied up. My legs and lungs burned as we finally fell panting into Dr. Jekyll's office.

———————

Henry and I made our way back to the boardinghouse in the pouring rain and in silence. When we arrived, both soaked to the bone, we shrugged out of our coats and hung them on a line stretched across the hearth in my room.

Henry's frame was visible through his nearly translucent shirt as he lowered himself into a chair. He rolled the sleeves to his elbows, exposing the smooth brown skin of his forearms. I looked away, afraid that my expression would betray me. I spread my notes from the day's classes out on the floor and shuffled them about, trying to put my mind elsewhere.

Henry stared into the fire, deep in his thoughts. In the weeks since our first meeting, I'd seen that he was prone to this kind of behavior—lost in his own head, staring off into the distance.

"Do you want to talk?" I asked.

Henry sighed. "I am not one to question my father's work, but I cannot set this aside."

"Is it not common to experiment with dead bodies?" The thought made me ill, but it was a known fact.

"Yes, but it seemed as if he were doing it in secret." Henry readjusted himself in the chair. "One of the things my father is very strict about is note-taking. He is meticulous in his documentation, and yet he asked that man not to record his findings. Why?"

"I have no idea," I said. "It does seem odd."

Henry shook his head. I didn't think he would elaborate further, but he took a deep breath and looked at me. "I was thinking of my father and that business with Sir Hastings. My father is a proud man, but he has earned it. He's smarter than Sir Hastings will ever be, and still Hastings would see my father groveling before him."

"My father would say that groveling is a valid path to respect."

Henry tilted his head, and a fire I so rarely saw in him flared up. "Would he?"

"I didn't say I agreed with him," I said quickly. "I've told you about my father and all of his training. He thinks that if he had not been so openly bitter about his rejection from the medical institutions in London, he may have had a better chance at gaining employment there."

Henry returned his gaze to the fire.

"My father thinks you can smile and 'yes, sir' your way to success," I continued. "That even if the opportunities don't materialize, well, at least you'll be viewed as a respectable person." Even as I spoke the words, I knew them to be wholly untrue. How my father had managed to convince himself of this was beyond my understanding. "If he had seen what happened between your father and Sir Hastings, he would have said that bowing to men like Hastings will allow us to be seen as grateful."

"Grateful for what?" Henry asked. "I don't see Hastings demanding submission of other professors."

"You understand why," I said.

Henry nodded. "Indeed, I do." He moved from the chair to the floor and stretched out in front of the fire, crossing his legs and folding his arms behind his head. His damp shirt was mostly dry and had come up around his waist, exposing his belly. I did not look away.

"Tell me, Gabriel . . . what do you want most in this world?"

I laughed before I could stop myself.

He turned to me and raised an eyebrow. "What's funny?"

"Nothing, I—I just never think of things like that."

That wasn't the truth at all. What I wanted in that moment was only him. I tried to think of an answer that wouldn't send me running from the room in sheer embarrassment but that would still be true enough for him to understand my meaning.

"What I want and what I'm allowed because of . . ." I trailed off, leaving the words unspoken, my heart threatening to punch its way out of my chest.

"Because of what?" Henry softly prodded.

I dared a glance at his face and found his gentle gaze. I still could not bring myself to say it. "It's nothing."

"Nothing? Hmm." Henry gazed up at the ceiling. "When you're ready to stop lying to me, I'll be here to listen."

Could this really be so easy? Could I share with him the things I'd kept so close? He seemed already to understand that we shared some unspoken kinship, and not just because we had difficult fathers and were walking paths that most of the waking world would see us trampled on—there was something else.

Henry took a deep breath. "What am I under this exterior, Gabriel? Who am I when everything else falls away?"

"You're Henry," I said. "Just Henry."

"And is that enough?" Henry asked.

"For who?" I measured my words so that there would be no confusion. "For the world?" I shook my head. "I don't think we should measure ourselves by what the world thinks of us."

"Then what do we measure ourselves by?"

I thought for a moment. "I wish you could see yourself through my eyes."

Henry angled his head toward me. "What would I see?"

I gripped my trembling hands together in front of me. "A quiet boy with a beautiful face. Someone who wants nothing more than to be seen for exactly who he is."

"Yes," Henry said in a whisper. "I want to be seen, and if I could be seen by you, well . . ."

"I see you, Henry," I said.

By the light of the fire, as Henry and I sat with only the steady drum of rain on the rooftop accompanying us, he stretched out his open hand and I took it, interlacing his fingers with mine.

CHAPTER 4

1884

WE'D BOTH TURNED SIXTEEN OVER THE SUMMER AND EXCHANGED so many letters in our time apart that I had to secret them in a trunk in the attic instead of between the folds of my mattress, where their growing number made it impossible to sleep comfortably. I wanted to bring them with me as I traveled back to London for my second year of study, but there wasn't room.

I'd brought with me the letters that mattered most—the ones where Henry addressed me as his "dearest Gabriel," where he spoke of his desire to see me again face-to-face and how that day would be joyful. He spoke of other desires, things that made my head swim with thoughts that I could confess to no one. He said nothing of his father's experiments or of what we had discovered beneath the London School, though I suspected it was not often far from his mind.

The day had finally come for Henry and me to be reunited, and I settled into my old room at Miss Laurie's and waited impatiently for him to arrive.

Every time the door opened, I raced to the top of the stairs.

There were many familiar faces, but it wasn't until the sun was almost set that Henry arrived. When I saw him for the first time after a long summer apart, I was undone.

He was taller, and his shoulders were broader, but his smile was exactly the way I remembered it. The same smile that had been emblazoned in my mind all these long months was now right in front of me.

Henry climbed the stairs, and as he looked up and caught sight of me he grinned. If I had not been holding on to the rail, I would have tumbled straight down the steps. I reached for him, but he stopped. He looked at me with an expression I'd never seen directed at me before. There was fear in his eyes—a look that told me I'd overstepped.

I immediately stepped back, shoving my hands in my pockets. Henry glanced back over his shoulder; Miss Laurie and the other boys had moved into the kitchen. When he was sure we weren't being observed, Henry took my hand and ushered me into my room, closing the door behind us.

He pressed in close to me but kept his gaze downcast, speaking in a voice that had dropped an octave since the last time I heard it. "It's very good to see you."

My heart fluttered. "I've been driving myself mad waiting for you. What took you so long?"

Henry sighed. "I meant to be here at dawn to make sure I was already settled when you arrived, but my father kept me for quite a while. He's long-winded, as I'm sure you're aware."

I chuckled. "Yes. Sitting in his class for an entire year showcased that perfectly."

Henry laughed, and it made the heat rise in my face. He pressed his forehead gently against mine and a long, slow breath escaped his lips. "I have missed you, Gabriel."

I took his hand and brought it to my chest, just over my heart. "You're never far from me."

"Can I ask you something?" Henry asked.

"Anything."

Henry's gaze darted around the room. "The letters we exchanged. Where are they?"

It was not the question I was expecting. "I left them at home," I said. "Hidden."

Henry let out a long, slow breath and gripped my hand.

"I did bring a few with me, though," I said.

Henry stared at me. "May I see them?"

I shrugged, and even though I never wanted to be parted from him ever again, I broke his grip and went to my bag to fish out the letters. Henry held out his hand and I gave them to him.

"I'm here now," he said. "We can say aloud all the things we've exchanged in these pages."

"Can we?" I asked. "Those letters are very dear to me."

The muscle in his temple flexed as if he were clenching his jaw. "We must be careful. You have no idea——" He stopped short and, in one swift motion, tossed the letters into the fire.

"Henry!" I raced to the hearth as if I could somehow save

the paper from being consumed, but it was already too late. The flames licked the pages, charring their edges and rendering them to ash in seconds. "Why would you do that?"

Henry gently took me by the arms and turned me around to face him. "If I am being too forward, please tell me, but I had assumed you'd prefer to hear me speak these things to you instead of reading them on paper."

"Yes, of course, but—"

Henry gently slid his hands down my arms until our hands were almost touching. "You understand how dangerous this will be. I know you do, otherwise you wouldn't have hidden the letters. I burned the ones you wrote to me."

I stared into his face.

"I burned them, but not before I memorized every line, every loop and curl of your terrible handwriting. I can recite them by date. They are not lost, but they now exist only where I can access them. Do you understand?"

I did, and as I thought on it, all I could see was my father's face in my head—his eyes burning with anger and then fear and then pity. It was the sole reason he had pushed me so hard into the field of medicine. It was a respectable profession, something he hoped I would become lost in. He couldn't have known what I would find there—the tenuous but all-consuming connection with my dear Henry, and how I wanted to be lost in nothing but his arms.

We fell into a routine. Classes in the morning and into the early afternoon, walks in the park when time permitted, and lunch in the courtyard.

One afternoon, Henry met me in the front room of the boardinghouse and handed me a piece of paper. I looked it over and found it to be an advertisement for a traveling circus that was being held in Sanger's Grand Amphitheatre. The creased paper showed an elephant walking a tightrope, assisted by a clown in a polka-dotted outfit. Bold black lettering stretched across the page:

SANGER'S GRAND AMPHITHEATRE

SOMETHING NEW UNDER THE SUN TWICE DAILY

SHOWCASING BLONDIN! THE GREATEST PERFORMING ELEPHANT IN THE WORLD!

"I am weary, Gabriel," Henry said. "Let's have some fun."

His eyes were alight, and still what he'd said troubled me. *I am weary*.

"Well?" Henry asked quietly. "Are you up for it?"

I nodded, and Henry raced off to change his clothes.

Sanger's Grand Amphitheatre sat on London's Westminster Bridge Road. When we arrived, the sun had ducked out of sight and the dark of nighttime closed in around us, but the festivities continued on. Outside the building people milled about. A man played a lively tune and some people danced, others drank. An atmosphere of anticipation permeated the air as a man in a bright red jacket with gleaming black buttons and a tall, black top hat emerged from the entryway of the amphitheater. He climbed a pedestal and brought a speaking trumpet to his mouth.

"Come one! Come all! My name is Pablo Fanque, and I welcome you to the grandest night of the season!"

In the crush of people, I found Henry's hand and grasped it tight. I looked into his face and his wide smile lit me up inside. We pressed forward as the man who called himself Pablo Fanque tipped his hat and ushered us through the grand entryway.

Inside, a crystal chandelier hung from the ceiling, directly above a large circular ring enclosing a dirt floor. Four tiers of seating in the round soared high above our heads, and patrons hung over the balconies, whooping and hollering as Pablo Fanque came to the center of the ring. In one bounding leap, he positioned himself atop a narrow platform.

We'd arrived too late to find seating on the upper tiers, so I pressed my hand to Henry's back and guided him to a spot by the rail on the lowest level.

"Utterson?" a voice asked suddenly.

At the rail was a familiar face—Lanyon. An upperclassman at the London School and a full two years older than Henry and me, he often palled around with my cousin Enfield in his off hours. We had only interacted a handful of times, but he'd always been kind. He smiled warmly and pushed aside his companions to make room for us.

"It's good to see you," Lanyon said. He eyed Henry. "And you as well, Jekyll."

Henry nodded, and I stood at the rail between him and Lanyon.

"This is shaping up to be quite a spectacle," Lanyon said, running his hand over his chin. "I was regretting allowing my cousin and his friends to drag me here, but now I'm very glad they did."

I looked at him, and he raised one finely shaped brow. Henry was staring into the center of the ring, and I was glad because my face flushed hot.

"Don't get yourself worked up," one of Lanyon's companions said to him. "Doctor said you're meant to be resting. We shouldn't even be here."

"Are you ill?" I asked.

Lanyon waved his hand dismissively. "My heart. I'm supposed to be keeping it beating in a slow, steady rhythm. But then you show up and well, there's not much I can do to keep it steady in your presence."

I was taken aback but I suddenly began to question any trivial interaction I'd ever had with him. I had clearly been so distracted by my adoration of Henry that I hadn't been able to see anyone else.

"Let us begin!" the ringmaster announced.

I was happy for the distraction. The ringmaster introduced a series of performers; a woman in a cream-colored costume walked a tightrope high over the ground as a troupe of clowns juggled sticks, some of which were on fire. With each new act, Henry and I clapped and cheered when we were prompted, and stayed absolutely silent when a young girl balanced atop another's shoulders, both of them balanced on a large canvas ball.

"This is magnificent," Henry said.

There were so many people crowded around that no one seemed to notice our intertwined hands, our shoulders pressing against one another. The heat, the smell of hundreds of warm bodies—under any other circumstances it would have been a miserable situation, but it was all worth it for the anonymity we enjoyed in the crowd.

"And now, if you would be so kind as to dim the lights," said the ringmaster.

Someone put out several of the torches, and a hush fell over the crowd. The amphitheater became shadowy and still.

The ringmaster removed his hat and pressed it to his chest. "Ladies and gentlemen, friends and foes. You have seen a great many acts this night and I hope you enjoyed them all, but now

I present to you something unlike anything you've seen before." The rest of the torchlight was extinguished, and then a beam of brilliant light streamed from somewhere over our heads, illuminating a crouched figure near the rear of the performance area.

A fiddle began to play a slow, somber tune in notes that felt wrong. I tightened my grip on Henry's hand and he pressed close to me. The figure rose up and only then did I realize it was a person. But their face was covered by a mask of some sort. It looked much like a human face—eyes, nose, and a wide, smiling mouth showing teeth—but it was made of some painted material. The only parts of the performer visible were their shining eyes. The figure contorted their body, twisting and turning around. I stepped back from the rail.

A woman gasped as the figure approached the rail in front of her and bent their back so that their hands and feet were on the ground at the same time. Not a moment later the woman fainted.

I could not take my eyes off the mask—the face rendered there was smiling, but it gave no feeling of comfort. It was not like the clowns who'd come out with their painted faces and bumbling ruckus of a routine.

Suddenly the figure scampered over and stood directly in front of Henry.

It was only then that I realized he was gripping the rail, and sweat had gathered on his furrowed brow.

The strange performer stood in front of him and then, in the blink of an eye, whipped their head around, revealing a second mask plastered on the back of their head. This was no smiling human face—it had large yellow eyes painted on, a gaping hideous mouth with thin lips, and a blackened tongue.

Henry stumbled back and crashed into me. I gripped his jacket and tried to steady him, but soon realized he wasn't trying to right himself; he was trying to run—to escape.

Lanyon caught Henry by the arm. "Are you all right, Jekyll? You look like you've seen a ghost."

Henry broke his grip and pushed past me. I barely managed to keep my own feet under me as he careened through a mostly silent crowd of onlookers who seemed unsure of what to make of the circus act. I shoved my way through the crowd and followed Henry out into the street, but he didn't stop.

"Henry!" I called as he dashed through the parked carriages and horses and into a park directly across the street.

When I finally caught up, I found him doubled over, his hands on his knees, chest heaving.

I gently rested my hand on his back. "Are you all right?"

Still trembling, he straightened and looked at me. His skin had a sickly pallor to it, and his eyes were wild and wet. "No," he said. "I—I don't know."

A fog had rolled in and laid across the ground like an undulating blanket of gray. Lamplight lit the small green space, and music wafted in from somewhere along Westminster Bridge Road. A slow tune, but nothing like the terrible music that had played as the performer in their dual masks stalked the amphi-theater. As I attempted to console a shaken Henry, little dots of light danced in the fog.

"Henry," I said. "Henry, look."

Henry glanced up as dozens of pinpricks of yellow light tum-bled through the dark.

"Fireflies," Henry said. He inhaled deeply and let his shoul-ders relax. "They shouldn't be out this time of year."

I'd never seen fireflies in the city. In the countryside they were everywhere. A pang of homesickness gripped my chest. I watched the lights dance and soon found myself reaching for Henry, who, after a quick glance, slipped his hand into mine.

"What happened in there?" I asked. "You looked so frightened."

Henry peered into the dark as more and more fireflies descended from the surrounding trees, filling the mist with an ethereal glow.

He shook his head. "I was scared. I'd never seen anything like that before. The mask, it . . . unsettled me."

I leaned on his shoulder. "Let's not speak of it. Let's just watch these fireflies and pretend we never saw it."

"I wish it were that easy," Henry said. "To just close my eyes and not see the terrible thing that's staring me in the face . . ."

I turned to him. "Henry—"

He pressed his hand to the side of my face. "I don't want to talk about it, if that's all right?"

I nodded, losing myself in the warmth of his touch. The music still played and the warm glow of the damp fog wrapped itself around us. Henry slipped his hand around my waist and began to sway with the music.

"Henry, I'm sorry, but I can't dance. I'm awful at it."

He laughed and pulled me closer. "It's easy. Just follow my lead."

I stumbled over my own feet, but Henry didn't miss a single step. As the fiddler in the distance began another tune, I began to pick up the movements.

Suddenly Henry stopped, squaring his shoulders with mine.

"I'm very bad at this—" I said.

Henry slipped his hand under my chin and pulled my face close to his, pressing his lips against mine.

Everything else disappeared. Nothing else mattered. It was only us and the fireflies and the night.

CHAPTER 5

MOTHER AND FATHER

A WEEK LATER, HENRY AND I MADE OUR WAY TO DR. JEKYLL'S classroom in the early morning, but as we approached the double doors that led to the operating theater, we found our classmates were gathered outside, blocking the way. They pushed and shoved each other, jockeying for a better view through the small rectangular windows. Samuel Riser—one of the upperclassmen who always seemed to be cleaning blackboards as punishment for rule-breaking—pushed his way to the front of the crowd.

"Get back!" Samuel shouted. "I want to see him get put out."

"See who get put out?" Henry asked in a whisper.

Everyone moved off to the side long enough for Henry to take their place at the window. His mouth fell open and a look of utter confusion washed over his face. He backed away from the door and looked down at the floor, shaking his head.

"Don't look so shocked," Samuel said. "It was only a matter of time."

"What's happening?" I asked.

Lanyon made his way toward me, his brow furrowed, his gaze narrow. "This is a complete farce. Sir Hastings is despicable."

I had no doubt about that, but I still didn't understand what all the commotion was about.

The double doors suddenly flew open, knocking several students back. Dr. Jekyll stumbled out carrying a wooden crate full of test tubes and glass vials.

"You will not set one foot off this campus with materials that belong to the institution!" Sir Hastings screamed, tripping along behind him.

Henry's father turned on his heel. "Your patrons make it explicit that their money is not to go toward my classes in any way. My god, Hastings, have you attended a single board meeting? Or are you happy to remain ignorant?"

Sir Hastings looked as if he might actually explode. "How dare you speak to me this way!"

"As I am no longer in your employ, I'll speak to you in the way that seems most appropriate," Dr. Jekyll snapped. "I will be removing my materials, all of which were purchased with my own funds. I will continue my studies elsewhere."

"Your studies? Your fringe science? Jekyll, you fool! Go! Take your tools and hide yourself away. It's what a disgrace such as yourself deserves!"

"Father," Henry began, but Dr. Jekyll took him roughly by the arm, cutting him off mid-sentence.

"Come straight home at the end of the day." He let go of Henry and stormed off as Sir Hastings fumed.

Samuel and his friends spoke in hushed whispers, laughing among themselves. Lanyon leaned close to me.

"Henry does not look well," he said. "You should tend to him but please, if there's anything I can do, do not hesitate to ask." He gently squeezed my arm and then left.

I'd seen much more of Lanyon on campus since the circus, but I was unsure if that was because he was seeking me out or simple coincidence. His distrust of Sir Hastings and concern for Henry gave me some hope that I had found another ally.

Henry looked like he might collapse under the weight of the embarrassment. I took him by the elbow and pulled him into the operating theater, toward his father's office. We went in and I closed the door as Henry slumped down in the chair and rested his head on his arms on top of the small desk.

"What is going on?" I asked.

Henry pressed his forehead into the desk as his body trembled. "My father has been working very hard for this institution for the better part of ten years. He's always been undervalued. Look at this office. Look at where he's forced to teach." He sighed. "Sir Hastings has been accusing my father of stealing since the summer."

I remembered the way Sir Hastings had burst into our classroom the previous year, demanding to know what had become of a shipment of supplies.

"That's a very serious claim," I said.

"It's not a claim," Henry said with a heavy sigh. "It's true."

I was struck silent. I moved closer to the desk. "Your father has been stealing from the university?"

"The same way they steal from everyone else," Henry said. "His colleagues steal his research and pass it off as their own. They charge my father triple the amount of tuition for me to attend, thinking he could never afford it, and when he does, they're so disappointed their plans have failed they take every opportunity to make his life a living hell."

I gently put my hand on Jekyll's shoulder. I didn't know what to say.

"My father would do anything for me," said Henry. "He wants nothing except for me to succeed where he thinks he's failed."

I understood that all too well.

Henry pushed his chair back and stood up. "Meet me in the courtyard after class." He brushed past me and turned his head just enough to give me a warm smile. "Please?"

"Of course."

He left without another word.

I stood alone in the disarray of Dr. Jekyll's office. There were papers and books scattered about the floor. He must have grabbed only what he could carry. On his desk there was a notebook lying open with his nearly illegible handwriting covering every inch of it. I didn't recognize much of the language used—

scientific terms I was not familiar with—and there were few drawings to illustrate whatever formulations he was obsessing over. I turned the pages and came across a lifelike drawing of Henry near the back.

Rendered from the shoulders up in black and white, Henry's smiling face beamed up at me from the page. Even in ink on paper his expression stirred something deep inside me. I wondered if Dr. Jekyll would mind if I kept the drawing for myself. I ran my hand over the paper and noticed a series of numbers, letters, and symbols—equations—at the bottom of the page. In a neat scrawl was a sentence I assumed was writing in Dr. Jekyll's own hand . . . *We cannot escape the nature of man's duality, but we can control its monstrous urges.*

———

In the courtyard, Henry stood in the shade of a towering silver maple, his jacket draped over his shoulder. The sun was beaming down on him, a short break in the usual gloom.

"Walk with me?" he asked.

I smiled at him. "You're asking me? You know there is nothing you could ask of me that I would not do."

"I want to take you home with me," Henry said.

I stopped in my tracks.

Henry's brow pushed together. "Unless you don't want to go," he said. "Of course you don't have to if you don't want to."

"No. I want to, I just—" I stepped closer to him. "Do your parents know about us?"

"Yes," he said, his tone flat.

I was at a loss. "You told them?"

"I could not hide from my father. But just because he knows does not mean he accepts it. That's something different altogether."

"And your mother?"

He kept his gaze on the road ahead of us. "She both knows and accepts, but ask her what it's like to say that out loud in my father's presence."

We traversed the London streets and came upon the Jekyll estate at 28 Leicester Square. Though large, enclosing nearly half a city block, it sat amid a sinister collection of buildings. Rot had seeped into the wood of all the residences that lined the street, but their owners tried very hard not to let it show. The Jekyll home was no different. The exterior was worn with age. Layers of chipped paint covered the shutters, and the front door was a patchwork of various woods—planks and slivers replaced one at a time instead of all at once. The surrounding wall, a six-foot brick-and-mortar structure, had been repaired so many times I wondered if any part of the original still remained. The front door of the home faced the street, surrounded by a high wall enclosing what I could just make out to be a garden and another large building. Henry mounted the front steps and waved me inside.

"Mother?" he called as he closed the door behind me.

The house was massive, and while it had clearly seen better days, it was a palace compared to the boardinghouse. It was warm and smelled of fresh flowers and burning firewood. There were three large rooms off the main hall and a kitchen near the rear that—from the sounds of clanking pots and the smell of fresh bread—was bustling.

I eyed the large painting of a stern-looking man in a blue suit that hung in the entryway. Dr. Jekyll's familiar check-patterned coat hung from a nearby coatrack; an assortment of walking canes, one with a handle in the shape of an eagle's head, stood in the corner.

A tall woman in a gray dress swept up to us. She embraced Henry and looked him over with the type of discerning gaze that told me she was his mother.

"You've already heard about your father, then?" she asked.

Henry nodded.

His mother turned her attention to me, and then back to Henry for a split second longer than she needed to. She pressed her hand over her heart and took Henry's hand in hers, something unspoken passing between them. His mother's gaze flitted to the back door, then down to the floor as she seemed to get lost in her own thoughts.

"Mother, this is Gabriel Utterson. He's staying in the boardinghouse, too. We have most of our classes together."

She shook herself out of her own head and stepped toward

me. She rested her hands on my shoulders. Her eyes were the same chestnut brown as Henry's, her dark, coily hair streaked with gray and folded into a braided halo.

"It's very good to meet you," she said. "My Henry has exchanged so many letters with you, I feel as if we already know each other."

My eyes grew wide, my heart nearly leaping out of my chest.

"Oh, but I haven't read them," she said quickly, looking away from me. "I would never. No. I just pass them through the post or deliver them to him when they arrive."

She patted me on the shoulder, and I had to keep myself from asking Henry right then why—if his parents were at least somewhat aware of his feelings for me—did he feel the need to burn my letters.

"Where's Father?" Henry asked.

His mother glanced toward the back door again. "Where he always is."

She gave Henry a kiss on the cheek and disappeared into the kitchen.

"He's in his laboratory," Henry said quietly. "Lately he's been taking meals there, sometimes sleeping there, too. It's stressful for my mother."

"Why does he spend so much time there?" I asked.

Henry stepped into the front room and sat down on a wide, evergreen chaise. He leaned his head back, and the dappled light filtering through the front window illuminated his troubled expression.

"He is trying very hard to continue his work. The facilities at the university were much more convenient. I think he's trying to replicate the same working environment in his own lab. It will take time, but I'm sure when he's done I'll see more of him."

He didn't make it sound like that was something he really wanted.

"Does your father have any recourse at the university? Can he appeal the firing?"

"On what grounds?" Henry asked. "He did what they've accused him of. He can't admit it, but he also can't deny it. Not fully."

"And there are no legal options?" I tried to think of anything that might help Dr. Jekyll regain his position. I was pained by the realization that if I'd gone to study law the way I wanted to, I might have had some better idea of what options were available.

The entire situation—Dr. Jekyll's firing, the strain it would inevitably put on Henry's already troubled mother—seemed avoidable, if only Henry's father had an advocate.

CHAPTER 6

Professor Kingston Knows

Three weeks went by. Dr. Jekyll was replaced by another professor who was given a proper classroom in the upper hall and a big, comfortable office. Dr. Jekyll's name was erased from the record, the faculty register, and the office at the back of the operating theater.

One afternoon, as Henry and I took our seats for our anatomy lesson, Samuel sauntered over and leaned on the desk.

"How's your father, Henry?" Sweat dampened Samuel's collar, and his red cheeks against his pale skin made him look sick.

Henry gritted his teeth and his nostrils flared. "He's well."

"Glad to hear it," Samuel said. "When you see him, could you ask him if he's seen any of our supplies? Another batch has gone missing and he seemed just desperate enough to have taken them."

Uproarious laughter erupted as Samuel's friends closed in around us.

"My father is a respectable man," Henry seethed. "Too bad the same can't be said for yours."

A hush fell over the classroom, and the reddish hue of Samuel's cheeks spread until it covered his neck. "What did you just say to me?"

Henry lifted his chin and made eye contact with Samuel. For a split second, I didn't recognize the expression on Henry's face. He was so rarely moved to anger.

Before Henry could say another word, Samuel seized him by the shirtfront and wrenched him to his feet. I grabbed hold of Samuel's coat, but his friends clamped their hands down on my arms and shoulders, twisting my arms behind me.

Professor Kingston entered the room and glanced over the scene. "Take your seats," he said.

Samuel hesitated.

"I will not repeat myself," Professor Kingston said.

Samuel released Henry; he fell back into his chair. His friends shoved me roughly to the side, and I retook my seat as they made their way back to their own. Henry just stared into his lap.

The lesson proceeded, but Henry didn't take a single note. He sat there with his head down, shoulders slumped forward the entire class. When the bell cut through the air nearly an hour later, I stood and gathered our things.

"Ignore Samuel," I said, slinging Henry's bag over my shoulder and arranging his books in a neat stack. "He's not worth being upset over."

Henry shook his head.

"Mr. Jekyll," Professor Kingston said as the last of the other students filed out. "Might I have a word?" He glanced at me. "Alone."

I took our things and left. Professor Kingston pulled the door closed but it didn't latch, staying open just wide enough for their conversation to drift out. I pressed my back against the wall and waited.

"Your marks have gotten steadily worse over the past several weeks," Professor Kingston said. "And while I'm sure it must have something to do with your father's dismissal, I am beginning to question your suitability for this institution."

"Hasn't that always been in question?" Henry asked.

Professor Kingston huffed. "You're astute. You would think a young man of your intelligence would understand that failing marks reflect poorly on you."

Henry didn't respond.

I was confused. Henry was smart. More than smart—he was *brilliant*. It didn't make sense that he was failing *any* class, much less anatomy, at which he'd always excelled.

"This will be your one and only warning, Mr. Jekyll."

A chair scraped across the floor and Henry emerged a moment later, his eyes brimming with tears. But he refused to let them spill over as he took his bag and books from me.

I put my hand on his shoulder. "What can I do to help?" I asked. "You're usually the one helping me, but if there's anything I can do to help get your studies back on track—"

"I don't care if they're on the track or off it," he said, turning away. "Neither do they."

I moved to follow him, but he stopped.

"I need a moment, Gabriel. Alone."

I tried not to let the hurt show on my face. "Of course."

Henry walked away, his shoulders rolled forward, his head down. He didn't have to say anything for me to know that he was hurting. I couldn't stand it.

The classroom door swung open and Professor Kingston stepped in front of me. "I'm glad you're still here. Something told me you would be. Come in for a moment."

He steered me back into the classroom and closed the door. Again, it didn't latch fully.

I stood with my back to the door, and Professor Kingston took a seat behind his desk. "You've done exceptionally well here, Mr. Utterson. You're such a smart young man, it makes me wonder . . ." He trailed off, staring out the open window.

"Wonder what, sir?"

Professor Kingston smiled and folded his hands together on top of his desk. "This is a delicate subject, Mr. Utterson. So delicate that I hesitate to elaborate in too much detail. But I find myself pitying you."

My stomach twisted itself into a knot, a rush of heat coursing through me. I avoided his eyes.

"Your reaction tells me that I'm onto something," Professor Kingston said. "Let me be plain—I see the way you and Mr. Jekyll lean on each other. There is a fellowship there, is there not?"

My heart thudded in my chest. I gripped the straps of my bag, my palms sweaty.

"Jekyll is my friend," I whispered.

Professor Kingston leaned forward. "Your very dearest one?"

I said nothing.

"Sir Hastings shared with me that your father wishes you to practice medicine. While that path is not what I would recommend for a young man of your station, it's a father's right to ask what they will of their children. If you want to honor him—if you want to save him any sort of scandal—you'd do well to distance yourself from Mr. Jekyll and focus on your lessons."

I glanced up at him and found in his face an expression of pity.

"I see in you something I once saw in myself," he said quietly. "But were it not for someone taking me aside and imparting to me the very same things I am trying to impart to you, I would not be here, in this position at this very prestigious institution. Do you understand what I'm saying to you, Mr. Utterson?"

"I—I don't know what you're implying but—"

"Do better," Professor Kingston said.

"What?" I asked.

"You'll need to work on your technique, because it's clear as day that you're lying." He sighed and leaned back in his chair. "You are nowhere near as subtle as you must be. Say you don't want him, and make me believe it."

My chest felt tight. I couldn't speak.

"Go on, then," Professor Kingston pressed. "Say it. Out loud."

"What do you want me to say?"

"Tell me the speculation running rampant among your classmates is absurd and that you're offended at the very notion of being romantically involved with Jekyll. If you can't convince me, you'll convince no one else, and all your prospects will disappear before your very eyes. You'll disappoint your father, your family, everyone who ever knew you. You will be shunned."

His fingertips pressed into the top of his desk so forcefully, I thought he might gouge out splinters of the mahogany wood. "Go on. Convince me."

Hands trembling, I pulled at my collar. "I—"

"Hold your chin up," Professor Kingston snapped. "Stick out your chest. Say it like you mean it."

But I couldn't mean it. I *did* want Henry.

Professor Kingston sighed. "Practice it, Mr. Utterson. Say it until you believe it. One day you may even convince yourself that it's true, and that is the day you can truly be free from it." He leaned forward and leveled his gaze at me. "You're dismissed, Mr. Utterson."

I turned and rushed toward the door only to see Henry's stricken face peering through the window.

"I thought you'd gone," I said as I slipped into the hall.

"I wanted to tell you—I needed to say—" He stumbled over his words for a moment, then sighed so hard I feared he might collapse in on himself. "I can't go on this way."

My heart shuddered. "Henry, please—"

He shook his head. "Meet me in Hyde Park in an hour."

He touched my hand one last time, then left me.

CHAPTER 7

FIRST ENCOUNTER

A TUMBLING GRAY FOG BLANKETED HYDE PARK AS I RUSHED TO the footpath along the southern bank of the Serpentine. The path was nearly empty on days like this, when the gloom was all-consuming. The maple and ash trees had already turned—crimson and bronze leaves bled through the ashen damp like watercolors. Henry wasn't there yet, so I paced the well-worn path until my feet ached, waiting for him to arrive.

I didn't want this to be over. It had barely begun and yet somehow our classmates had sniffed us out like wolves to raw meat. They wanted a scandal. All Henry and I had ever done was tend to our own business, study together, walk in the park. They could let us be. But they wouldn't, and now we'd attracted the attention of Professor Kingston. His words echoed in my head: *You are nowhere near as subtle as you must be.*

I hadn't been *trying* to be subtle about my feelings for Henry. I hadn't been trying to be boastful, either. I was only trying to live.

The professors never demanded subtlety from the boys in

my year who chased the nursing students across the court-yard, pulling up their skirts and harassing them until they had to commission nuns from the campus rectory to accompany them to and from classes. There was no plea for modesty when Samuel and his friends said vulgar things about the institute's two secretaries—it was even encouraged by professors who had the same terrible thoughts running through their own minds.

Perhaps the pressure of it all was too much for my dear Henry. He had asked me more than once to keep my head down, to be aware of those around us—which sometimes felt impossible, because when I was with him, he was all I could see.

A rustling drew my attention, and Henry emerged from the gloom like a ghost.

I heaved a sigh of relief. "I was worried you wouldn't show."

I expected him to chuckle. He didn't. Instead, he kept his gaze fixed on the ground. "I needed to see you."

My stomach was set aflutter at those simple words.

"I'm sorry for what I said. I never want to hurt you, Gabriel."

I approached him slowly, but he took a step back.

"Please," I said. "Please don't pull away from me. I can't bear it."

Henry clasped his hands together in front of him and bit his bottom lip the way he did when he was upset. "Have you given any thought as to what *I* can bear?"

I waited for him to meet my gaze, but still he avoided it.

"I don't know what you mean," I said.

"Yes you do." He glanced up long enough for me to see the fear in his eyes. "We both know that there are very real consequences for what we are doing."

"We're not doing anything."

"Aren't we? What you feel for me, you think it can be overlooked?"

"Are you . . . Are you saying you don't feel the same things for me?" A terrible ache gripped my chest.

"I do," he said through gritted teeth and glassy eyes. "And it is the source of my greatest pain. How can that be?"

He moved closer to me. I stepped back, leaning against a tree as Henry pressed his chest against me. As the deepening mist surrounded us, he put his mouth to mine and I breathed him in, felt his heart pounding beneath my own frantic pulse. He rested his forehead on mine, his breath warm on my face.

"There is a part of me that wants only this," he murmured. "Only you. But——"

"But what?" I asked.

He glanced up and down the footpath, so unsure of himself. A look of utter sadness stretched across his face. "But I can't see a way through. Professor Kingston is suspicious. I heard everything he said to you and I hate it, but he's not wrong. The other students in our year have taken notice. My father believes it is yet another reason Sir Hastings fired him."

"Because of us?"

"It doesn't matter now. My father has offered me a chance to redeem myself."

"Redeem you for what? You didn't do anything wrong!"

He took a step back. "My mother has made arrangements for my things to be collected from the boardinghouse."

My head spun, a crush of fear threatening to overtake me. "I—I don't understand."

"You will," Henry said, his voice hollow and distant. "Or perhaps you won't. But trust me when I say it is for the best. There are things happening that may make this much easier for both of us. We can be free from this burden."

I could barely think straight. "Henry, what are you not telling me?"

He pressed his lips together and shook his head. "How do you not feel the weight of it? How can you look at me like that and not feel shame?"

A knot tightened in my throat. "I feel a great many things when I look at you, Henry. Shame is not among them."

It wasn't the entire truth. There was shame, but only because so many people in my life had insisted there should be.

"How is that possible?" Henry insisted. "How do you not see the looks and hear the whispers?"

"I do see it," I said. "I wish I didn't."

His breaths pumped out of him in gasps. It seemed to be taking everything in him not to cry or shout. He kept everything inside himself. "Then you agree that I—that *we*—cannot go on this way?"

"I agree. But not in the way you think," I said, choosing my words carefully. I feared he would bolt at any moment. "We can't go on this way, caring so much about what others think of us that we forget what is most important." I clutched the front of his coat. "You and me, Henry. That is what matters. That is *all* that matters."

"How do we hide from the people who will judge us?" he asked.

"We can't." I took his hand in mine and interlaced our fingers. "We still deserve to live, Henry. We still deserve a chance to be happy."

He pulled back from me. "Forget what I've said. Forget everything. I—I can't do this."

My heart splintered. "Please, don't go," I begged, the words feeling stuck in the dry hollow of my throat. I stepped toward him.

"Don't," he said, turning away. "Please don't."

And I watched Henry walk away from me.

All the months we'd spent in each other's company, all the words spoken in letters and in the fog when no one was watching . . .

My knees buckled, and I hit the dirt, kneeling there for a long time until Henry's silhouette was consumed by the fog.

———

I made my way to the boardinghouse in a daze. When I arrived, I went straight to Henry's room, but found it empty, his things already collected. Miss Laurie informed me that his bill had been paid up, with no indication that he'd be returning.

I sat in my room in silence for hours, unsure of what to do. Numb. Perhaps it was not too late to convince Henry that we could figure this out in a way that wouldn't hurt us both so. I could barely fathom the thought of not seeing him every day—of not sitting with him by the fire laughing at my terrible handwriting and my utter uselessness at arithmetic. A wave of desperation washed over me, and I scrambled out of my room and downstairs. I dashed out of the boardinghouse and imme- diately made my way to Leicester Square.

The lamplighters were making their rounds when I arrived on Henry's doorstep. The orange glow from their lamps beat back the gloom in perfect circles at the base of each post. I rang the bell and when no one answered I knocked. Even as neigh- bors retreated inside their houses for the night, I sat on Henry's front step, unable to drag myself away until I'd spoken to him.

The street was lulled into an uneasy quiet as the nighttime closed in. From the alleyway immediately beside the Jekyll res- idence, the rear door yawned open. I stilled myself, watch- ing for someone to emerge. Footsteps sounded on the damp pavement—heavy and halting. I held my breath and peered into the shadows. A ripple of apprehension washed over me, and I stood on shaky legs.

"Hello?" I called into the damp, dark night.

The fog shifted and something moved—a shadow cast by

someone standing just inside the alleyway. There was a noise—in and out. Breathing.

My heart punched against my ribs. I stepped down and angled my head. A figure was leaning up against the bricks.

"Who's there?" I asked.

A sharp intake of breath and then a low rumble, like a growl caught in someone's chest.

The front door to the Jekyll residence swung open, and I cried out and stumbled back as a warm light poured out into the street.

"Utterson?" Dr. Jekyll asked. He glanced toward the alley. "What are you doing here?"

I looked back toward the alley only to find it empty, the figure gone. I collected myself, convinced my anguish over Henry was having a terrible effect on my mind, and removed my cap.

"Dr. Jekyll, sir," I said. I was suddenly very aware that I hadn't thought this through. I had no prepared answers, only the fear and panic I felt that had driven me here.

"Henry isn't here," Dr. Jekyll said, as if he could read my thoughts. "He's been expelled and is taking it rather hard. He'll be gone for a while to gather himself."

"*Expelled*? What? When?"

Dr. Jekyll peered at me through his round spectacles. "You and Henry have become quite close. I'm surprised he didn't contact you straight away with the news. It only happened today and still . . ." He trailed off. "Perhaps the two of you are not as close as I'd assumed."

I gripped the railing in a feeble attempt to steady myself.

"I think it best you give Henry some time to get his thoughts together," Dr. Jekyll said. "I can assure you that his friendship with you is, indeed, very important to him. He's doing what he must to preserve that, but you'll need to allow him the time."

What he said didn't make sense to me. "I'm sorry, sir, but preserve our friendship? I don't follow your meaning."

"Don't you want to continue to be friends with Henry?"

I nodded. Of course I did. I wanted much more than that.

"And isn't that the most important thing? That you can do so without any . . . complications?"

I still did not entirely understand, but Dr. Jekyll came down the steps and clamped his heavy hand on my shoulder.

"Of course it is!" he said with a jovial, almost ecstatic, ring in his tone. I'd never seen him so enthusiastic. "It *is* the most important thing. You'd do well to remember that. Run along home now, Utterson. Henry will come to you when he's ready, and we will celebrate new beginnings together."

"I don't understand," I said.

Dr. Jekyll smiled but said nothing more before he retreated inside. The lights dimmed, plunging the stoop into darkness.

Now it made sense why Henry had been so upset. Why he hadn't told me that he'd been expelled was beyond me, but now that I knew, I hoped he would come to me in his own time.

The sinking dread I'd felt dissipated long enough for me to

realize I was out long past Miss Laurie's curfew and needed to return to the boardinghouse immediately. Before I turned off Leicester Square, I glanced back at the alleyway.

For a moment I thought I saw someone standing there, but as the fog rolled away, there was nothing.

———

"Breaking curfew is grounds for termination of our arrangement," Miss Laurie chided as I slipped into the boardinghouse. "But I'm going to let it pass because clearly you must have had a lapse in your normally stellar judgment."

She whipped her head around and stared at the other residents who'd come into the front room, likely hoping to see a show. But Miss Laurie didn't seem like she was in the mood for putting me out right at that moment.

"Don't any of the rest of you go getting ideas!" she shouted. "You'll be out in the street before you can blink!" She winked at me. "Supper, dear? Everything's on the table."

"I don't think I can eat," I said honestly.

"Ah well, sleep then." She reached into her apron and pulled out a sealed letter. "Left by Henry earlier. He said it should only be opened by you." She clicked her tongue behind her teeth. "I didn't like the look he had about him. Didn't like it one little bit."

As she shuffled off, I raced to my room and tore open the letter.

My Dearest Gabriel,

I am sorry for all you have endured on my behalf. Knowing you, you'll insist that it isn't my fault, but deep down I know you know it's the truth.

I cannot say goodbye to you in person. Things have transpired that cannot be undone, but I will write to you at my earliest convenience. The summer months will be long, but I choose to think of them as a test. And if I can endure it, I know we will be all the better for it.

You said to me that we deserve to live, Gabriel. And you're right. We do. So I will do what I must to ensure that can happen. I feel that with you, there is nothing I cannot do. I go toward this impossible task in hopes that our bond may yet survive it. Trust in me.

On a fully separate note, I think you should consider turning your attention to law. You and I have seen what Hastings thinks of us. Go and chase that dream of yours.

Ever yours,

Henry

I pressed the letter to my chest as if I were embracing Henry himself. What he had said to me in the park felt final; this letter gave me some glimmer of hope that it was not some terrible goodbye.

I knew I should burn the letter, but I could not. I slipped it under my mattress and fell into a restless, dreamless sleep.

When I woke, all I could think of were Henry's words. He knew better than anyone what my heart truly desired—besides him—was to practice law. He also knew full well that my father was dead set on my becoming a physician. I pictured enduring Sir Hastings's remarks, facing Professor Kingston's accusatory glances, and the thought drove me into a state of rage I'd never felt so keenly in all my life.

I was determined to make the decisions that were best for me, just as my brave Henry was doing right at this moment. He'd gone off to make a way for us. I didn't know how he'd accomplish it, but he had asked me to trust in him and I did. Now I needed to do my part.

I dressed, ate, and made my way to campus, set on informing Sir Hastings that I would not be attending the London School for Medical Studies a single day longer.

When I arrived at his office, his secretary smiled.

"Sir Hastings is expecting you," she said.

I stared at her, confused. "He is?"

She nodded and motioned to the heavy set of double doors that led into the office. I pushed them open and found myself in the company of not only Sir Hastings, but Professor Kingston and another man I'd seen on campus but did not know by name.

"Ah, Mr. Utterson," Sir Hastings said. "Come in and sit down. We have much to discuss."

Sir Hastings was seated behind his desk, while Professor Kingston sat in a winged-back chair in the corner. The other man stood by the fireplace and didn't even look up as I sat down.

"Your dear friend Henry Jekyll has been expelled," Sir Hastings said.

I nodded as my skin pricked up. I was in danger, and every part of me understood that terrible fact.

"He violated our school's morality code," Professor Kingston said.

It took everything in me not to scoff in their faces. I hadn't read the school's rules about morality, but I was certain every man in that room had violated it in some way.

Sir Hastings narrowed his eyes at me. "And it seems you are complicit, Mr. Utterson."

"Complicit in what?" I asked.

Sir Hastings and Professor Kingston exchanged glances.

"You'll be expelled," Sir Hastings said. "Your father will need to pay a fine for your . . . indiscretions. And you'll be barred from this campus."

I gripped the armrests until my hands ached. "That's not fair." I didn't want to be there, but I wanted to leave on my own terms. And I certainly didn't want my father to have to pay a penalty. "I can pay the fine if you'd permit me time to find work. Do not put this burden on my father."

"How very noble of you," the man by the fireplace said. He

turned and walked over to sit in the empty chair next to me. He smelled like cigar smoke and drink. The man stuck out his hand, and I shook it. "I'm Sir Danvers Carew. I own and operate a firm here on the grounds, specializing in medical law."

I didn't care.

"Seems you've gotten yourself into quite a predicament," Sir Carew continued. "Lucky for you, I think I might be able to be of some assistance."

I glanced up at him, but he kept his gaze locked on Sir Hastings. "You say he's intelligent."

Sir Hastings nodded. "Oh yes. It's a shame, really. So much talent and all of it trapped in this unfortunate visage."

They all chuckled, speaking about me as if I weren't sitting right there.

"And what of his father?" asked Sir Carew. "Is he heavily involved? You know that I don't like to be bothered when I'm working. That includes unwanted interference from kin."

"He lives far from London and is in no position to argue against any inquiry from you, Sir Carew," Sir Hastings assured him.

"I'll take him then," Sir Carew said. "But do him the courtesy of allowing him to disenroll. An expulsion on his record would do me considerable harm should someone look into his background. I can't have any of this reflect poorly on me."

"Of course," Sir Hastings said. "You're a saint, Danvers. Truly."

Sir Carew smiled and they chuckled together again.

"Am I to have no say in the matter?" I asked.

The three men went completely silent.

Sir Carew turned to me. "And what would you say if given the opportunity? Would you protest?" He laughed. "I'm saving you from a lifetime of embarrassment. You should be thankful—Sir Hastings is well within his rights to dismiss you outright." He reached over and put his hand on my knee. "No. You'll come clerk for me and you'll be grateful."

As Professor Kingston poured three glasses of self-congratulatory brandy, Sir Hastings leaned across the desk. "I'm sure you'll do very well with Sir Carew to guide you. He's been of great service to a number of unfortunate boys like yourself."

Sir Carew gave me a nod. This opportunity would allow me to learn the ins and outs of the law and save me from having to say I was expelled.

But the way Sir Carew had spoken to me, his hand on my knee, the way I felt as if I'd been acquired by this man . . . it all put a terrible twist in my gut.

PRESENT

CHAPTER 8

1885

My Dearest Henry,

I pray this letter finds you safe. Please, please write to me and tell me you are well. I asked my cousin Enfield to inquire about your boarding arrangements. I know your father prefers you to stay under his wing, but there is room at Miss Laurie's, should you wish to have some place for you to be . . . alone.

But when I received Enfield's response just this morning I was dismayed. I had hoped you would return to Miss Laurie's. I hope your absence is not because of the things left unsaid between us. The months apart have been long and I have had time to reflect on our last meeting, but I must confess that although I try to remember the words that were spoken, all I can envision is your smiling face.

I will arrive in London in two weeks' time. I will come to find you and we will remedy this. Trust in me, my dearest

Henry. They think they know our story, but I can assure you, they do not.

Always,

Gabriel

After the disastrous events of the fall, my father brought me home straight away and all through the winter and spring he had stressed to me the importance of this new opportunity. My work in Sir Carew's office was to begin in March and when the time came to return to London, I could not set aside a terrible, aching sense of dread.

Sir Carew sent my father a contract to sign, stating that he would pay a large fee if my services were not to his liking. He sent parcels full of notes and instructions detailing the work I would be conducting. He made it clear that I was to come to his office prepared and ready to oblige his every whim. My father failed to see any issue with the way Sir Carew lorded over me and firmly believed that if I smiled enough and said "Yes, sir" at the right moments to the right people, I could leverage this opportunity and perhaps convince myself that Carew actually respected me.

My father was certain of only one thing—my success hinged on the thoughts and feelings of others, and I was to chase that respectability like a dog chases its tail, even if all it ever did was lead me right back to where I started. I was told at every possible opportunity that I was to be thankful Sir Carew had opened his practice to me and allowed me to clerk for him.

A thin mist slicked the train's windows as it pulled into Euston Station. The whistle screamed and passengers began to move about, collecting their things, preparing to disembark. I tucked a letter I'd been holding in my breast pocket, its contents unread—because I was a coward. I'd written to Henry two weeks prior and his response arrived just one day ago.

I held his letter in my hand. I hadn't had the opportunity or the courage to open it yet. His letters of late had grown somber in their tone. I dared not imagine what that could mean for us both.

The train's whistle screamed again, this time with more urgency, cutting straight through my thoughts. I took my bag from the overhead storage compartment and waited as the first-class passengers filed out.

A tapping on the window drew my attention. My cousin Enfield was clinging to the outside of the car, pressing his nose against the glass. A woman with an angry red face wearing a hat topped with feathers and ribbons that looked much like a bird's nest scowled at him as she disembarked. I shooed Enfield away, laughing. When I finally shuffled off the train he caught me around the waist and nearly lifted me off the ground, squeezing the air out of me.

"Cousin!" he said, beaming. "I've been chased off the platform twice waiting for you." He set me down and looked me over. Enfield was a year older than me, and a head taller. He had arrived in the city the previous month and I was happy to have family close by. He was, as always, one of the very few people who knew everything there was to know about me and who held no judgment.

"Just the one bag?" he asked.

I nodded and he patted my shoulder.

"I've got extra," he said. "You can take whatever you need."

A silent understanding passed between us. My family was as well-off as we were allowed to be, but greasing Sir Carew's palms had left us with barely enough money to live, much less outfit me for my time in his office. The opportunity he had offered me did not come without a price. I shook my head and readjusted my bag on my shoulder.

I had three changes of clothes that I would keep meticulously cleaned and pressed, switching between them as needed. Enfield wasn't any better off in the city, but his mother—my aunt Clara—was a seamstress and could make a way out of no way when needed.

Enfield grabbed my bag from me and slung it across his back, draping his arm over my shoulder. "Let's go before they run us off again."

As we left the station, passing under the ode to Roman architecture, the great Euston Arch, and out into the cramped streets, the evening air was thick with sooty gray fog. The smell of food, coal smoke, and horse manure assaulted my senses with every shift of the breeze. It always took me a few days to acclimate. I'd been away from the city for nearly three months, and while I enjoyed the bustling cityscape much of the time, a pang of longing for the open air of the country settled in my chest. The feeling was reminiscent of another longing.

"Have you learned anything else about Henry?" I asked.

Enfield shook his head. "Only that he still hasn't made arrangements at the boardinghouse. He doesn't really need to, though, does he?"

No. He didn't need to stay there. His family had always been well-off enough to allow him to stay at their stately Leicester Square home. But Henry had stayed in the boardinghouse before—to be close to me. A ripple of unease coursed through me as I recalled his last letters.

"We can drop off my things and go round to Leicester Square."

Enfield eyed me carefully. "You don't want to rest? Eat?"

"No. I want to find Henry."

Enfield sighed and shrugged, slapping me hard on the back. "All right. Since you have your mind made up."

Enfield regaled me with stories about his latest entrepreneurial endeavor—he and a few friends had claimed an entire stretch of street in St. Anne where they swept away the filth and excrement so that rich men wouldn't have to get their shoes dirty. Enfield was very proud, and I was ready to applaud him as we emerged onto Leicester Square but lost my train of thought.

The Jekyll residence stood in the gloom like a slumbering beast. A group of young children played in the street—a girl of seven or eight pestered her brothers to let her swing a stick at a tattered canvas ball. They begrudgingly indulged her and with one swing, she knocked it halfway down the street. They immediately began to fight over whose team she'd be on. The girl, her dark coily hair braided in a crown around the top of her head, knees dotted with freshly healed scrapes, smiled triumphantly.

As the children whooped and hollered to each other, another noise sounded in the narrow street. I gazed up and down the cobbled way, expecting to see a carriage or horses, but was met with nothing but a slowly descending fog and the continued laughter and shouting of the children. The sound grew like thunder in the distance. I was the only one to hear it at first, but soon the children, Enfield, and I were all peering down the street. The noise edged closer until I was finally able to identify it—footsteps.

Running.

A man burst from the darkness in a fit of frenzied breaths. He barreled into the street, seemingly unaware of the small children in his path. The man, wild-eyed and frantic, trampled through them. He collided with the dark-haired little girl and their legs twisted together. They fell into a tangled heap and a loud crack split the air—the sound of a bone being knocked violently from its socket. The girl's bleating cries signaled to me that it was she who had been injured, not the man.

Her brothers gathered around her as the man scrambled to his feet and tensed as if he was about to run.

Enfield grabbed him by the wrist. "Look what you've done!" he shouted. "Now you're running away?"

A trio of men burst from the alley—a short, balding man in a cap, a taller, lanky man wearing a dark coat and tattered trousers, and a burly, stout man with a head of blond ringlets and eyebrows so pale they gave the impression that he had none at all.

Residents along the street descended upon the chaotic scene. The men from the alley pointed and yelled, looking wildly about. They spotted their man, the very same one responsible for the girl's injury. The group fell on him like wild dogs on a fresh kill, grabbing him by the collar of his jacket and shoving him back and forth between them. They looked as though they were about to tear him limb from limb. The anger in their eyes was personal, and it struck me as irrational. What we'd just seen was clearly an accident, and yet they pursued him with the kind of intensity better suited for a criminal.

I rushed to the girl's side to see if I could tend to her injury.

A woman in a long dress, apron tied around her waist, came out of a house nearby and knelt beside her. "Oh my god! What happened? Who did this?"

I glanced back at the man being restrained by the others. He wasn't struggling, only looking upon the scene in abject terror. I'd thought him an old man upon first seeing him; his hair was so white it was almost translucent. But as I watched him further, I saw his face was smooth, beardless. Not even scruff. He was a young man, which made the matter of his hair a little odd. I turned back to the girl, whose entire family had now gathered in the street.

Her leg was bent at an unnatural angle and she screamed as I palpitated her knee. My time as a student at the London School for Medical Studies was over, but I'd learned enough to recognize a dislocated joint when I saw it. I'd also learned a fair amount from my mother, who had to regularly pop her own bones back into place after arguments with her father in which much more than angry words were exchanged.

"Her knee is dislocated," I said. "I can fix it, but you'll need to hold her still. It will be quite painful."

An older man came out of the house, looked at the girl's leg, then put his hands on his knees as the color drained away from his face. He looked as if he might spill his guts onto the cobblestone at any moment.

"Oh, my poor girl," he groaned.

The woman in the apron, apparently the girl's mother, rolled her eyes and pushed up her sleeves. She gripped the girl's arms and lay across her, pinning her to the damp paving stones.

"Fix it," she said. "I'll hold her."

Taking the girl's lower leg in my hand and putting pressure on the outside of the deformed joint, I yanked hard. The bone popped into its proper place. The girl didn't make a sound; her big brown eyes rolled back and her entire frame went limp. Her mother cried out in her stead.

I took the girl's clammy hand in mine and counted the pulses against the faint ticks of my pocket watch. Her tiny chest rose and fell just as it should have.

"She'll be all right," I assured her mother. "Take her in and bind the knee tightly. Give her broth and a cool rag for her head. Call a doctor as soon as you're able."

She smiled and thanked me profusely. As the girl stirred, her brothers gathered her up and took her inside. Her father stayed behind, eyeing the man who had trampled his daughter with a seething hatred so palpable I could almost picture it rolling off him in waves.

"You did that to my daughter," the girl's father said angrily. "You ran her over and tried to flee?"

"It was an accident," the white-haired man said, his voice low and trembling. "I was being—" Before he could finish his sentence, one of the men who had him restrained punched him in the gut. He doubled over, a line of bloody spittle dripping from his bottom lip.

"We caught him for you," the stout man said as he delivered another punch to the man's ribs. "He was trying to run, but we got him!"

The three men exchanged glances, and I had a suspicion that they were not at all interested in making sure he was held accountable for the girl's injury.

"You were chasing him before he ran over the girl," I said, taking another look at the man. He tried to stand up but fell forward, wincing in pain. His lip was bloodied and his right eye was bloodshot, the skin around the socket ruddy and swollen.

"What happened to your eye?" I asked him.

He lifted his head and as his gaze settled on me, I felt a twist in the pit of my stomach. He was scared to death.

"Did you lot do this to him?" Enfield asked, eyeing the young man's injuries and rounding on the men who'd been chasing him.

The tall man squared his shoulders and marched up to my cousin, jamming his finger in his chest. "I'll not be questioned by the likes of you," the man said. "You'd do well to remember your place."

As if we could ever forget. As if they would ever let us.

We knew very well how we were looked at no matter what jobs we held or what schooling we'd had. Even this disheveled brute who'd been chasing a terrified young man through an alley—who smelled of drink and sweat, who'd offered not so much as a pitied glance at the poor girl who'd been run over—thought he was better than us because he was white and we were not. His threat, however, did not sit well with Enfield, and Enfield had never been shy about voicing his distaste for bullies.

My cousin removed his coat and tossed it on the ground. He

boxed for profit when he needed a little something extra in his pocket. My aunt Clara would have been devastated to know that, but in that moment, I was elated.

Enfield glowered down at the man, who took a step back and straightened out his own jacket.

"My problem's not with you," the man said.

"You're lucky that way," Enfield said, the hint of a smile on his lips.

As my cousin stood at the ready, I took a moment to get a better look at the young man. I realized he probably wasn't much older than me. Clean shaven, dark russet skin, large—but terrified—brown eyes. A mass of tight coils cut close around the edges and tinted the color of freshly fallen snow topped his head. He was the most extraordinary-looking person I'd ever seen, second only to my dear Henry.

"I can make it right," the young man said. "If you'll allow me to—"

"Shut up!" one of the other men said, delivering a blow to his cheek.

"Stop!" shouted the girl's father, sauntering over. "He can't tell me how he's going to make this right if he's bloodied up. Let him catch his breath."

The other men reluctantly loosened their grip on him.

The girl's father clasped his hands together. "You said you could make it right. I'm very curious to know how you're going to do that."

"I—I can pay you," the young man stammered. "Let me retrieve my check register and I can pay you."

The girl's father looked skeptical, but money is persuasive, and he had no doubt noticed the same things I had: The young man's shoes were polished to a high shine, his clothes were finely tailored, and his jacket was cut like it was made specifically for his broad frame. He was of means, and the girl's father fully intended to take advantage of that detail.

"How far do you need to go to fetch your register?" the girl's father asked.

"Just there." The young man gestured to a door near the rear of the Jekyll estate. "Please. Allow me to make amends."

The girl's father nodded and the young man rushed off. I held my breath as he approached the door. Surely he was mistaken. Maybe he was turned around from his encounter with the men and with the girl. There was no reason he should be able to enter the Jekyll residence at all, but much less from the rear door. To my surprise, he produced a key from his pocket and entered.

"Strange," I said quietly.

Not a few moments later, the young man reappeared. He marched up to the girl's father and put a paper check in his hand.

"It's drawn on Standard Bank and Trust. They'll honor it, I swear. I'm very sorry." The young man's voice was choked with emotion and he glanced toward the house where the girl's family resided. A shadow passed over his face. As the greedy men gathered around the girl's father, the young man with the white hair and dark eyes quickly turned and disappeared back into the Jekyll residence.

The girl's father looked down at the check, and the tall man in the coat huffed.

"You've been taken advantage of," said the short, balding man. He spit on the ground. "He's gotten away and you're left with nothing. Fool."

Enfield nudged his way in and glanced at the check. His eyes grew wide in the gloom.

"What is it?" I asked. The girl's father held the check in his hands like it was made of glass. I peered over his shoulder and immediately saw what had caused the look of utter astonishment plastered across his face: The check was for one hundred pounds, and was signed by Dr. Jekyll himself.

The girl's father quickly tucked it away and stepped back from me like I might try to relieve him of his compensation. He rushed inside, and even from the middle of the street I heard the locks on his door click.

Alone in the street with the men who'd been chasing the stranger, I suddenly felt too exposed. Equipped as Enfield was to deal with an opponent, it was three on two, and I didn't like those odds. Still, I couldn't get the image of the young man's frightened face out of my head.

"Why were you chasing that man?" I asked.

They all stared, and then the tall man with sandy-brown hair stepped toward me.

"No reason that concerns you," he said. He shoved me hard in the shoulder as he and the others brushed by. I had to grab hold of Enfield's shirt to keep him from punching the short blond man in the back of the head.

"Let them go," I said quietly.

"Why is Henry's father writing checks for that amount of money?" Enfield asked. He retrieved his coat and brushed it off, looking after the men with cold, unblinking eyes. "Shouldn't he want to come out and see what it was all about?"

"Apparently not," I said.

As the group of men faded into the encroaching darkness and a thick layer of fog pulled itself over the street like a blanket, I glanced up at the Jekyll residence. There had been only shadows before, but now a light flickered on, and a figure cloaked in darkness passed by the upper window.

CHAPTER 9

REMEMBER ME

ALL I COULD SEE WHEN I CLOSED MY EYES WAS THE YOUNG GIRL'S mangled leg, her face twisted in pain. And of course, the strange young man who had caused her injury. His terrified eyes left me deeply concerned for his safety. What happened to the girl had been a terrible accident, that was clear, but the men who had chased him from the alley had been out for blood.

Then there was the matter of his dealings with the Jekyll family—how easily he'd gone in and secured a check for a large sum of money, how he'd had a key that allowed him to come and go as he pleased. Henry hadn't mentioned this young man at all in any of our correspondence. It left me unsettled and stirred something envious deep inside me.

Since his expulsion, Henry had been a ghost. I hadn't seen him face-to-face at all. Dr. Jekyll had told me Henry would find his way back to me, but he still hadn't and I wondered how much longer I should wait before I went searching. After traveling back to my father's home, I had received a handful of letters from Henry, each one more distant and disconnected than the last. He spoke of his work, sometimes of his mother, but he rarely spoke of us, and my questions to him were always left unanswered.

Enfield reclined in a wicker chair Miss Laurie had placed in my room. She didn't care for the fact that I would be clerking for Sir Carew. She found him just as detestable as I did and informed me that should I decide to leave his employ, I would still have a warm bed and three hot meals a day. She had become something of a second mother to me, and I cared for her with that same affection.

"I've seen him before, you know," Enfield said. "That white-haired boy who trampled the girl. I've seen him around Leicester Square several times. My mother's doing some work for one of the families over there, mending school clothes for the children. I've seen that very same young man entering the rear door of the Jekyll residence on at least three separate occasions."

The Jekyll estate, being built in a sort of elongated rectangle, did have a rear entrance, but I was unsure of where exactly it led to.

Another thought entered my mind: This young man who seemed so wide-eyed, so vulnerable in that terrible moment when he realized what he'd done, was coming and going from the Jekyll residence as he pleased. Which meant my dear Henry must have known of him but was choosing to keep it a secret.

"Why does he use the back door?" I asked. "I can't imagine Dr. Jekyll just letting a stranger go in and out of his home at his leisure."

Enfield shrugged. "He's clearly not a stranger to Dr. Jekyll, Gabriel. Your guess is as good as mine, but I suspect it's because he doesn't want to be seen going through the front."

I couldn't imagine why it would matter. Who was this person and what business did he have with the Jekylls? A sudden stab of envy gripped my entire chest and I turned away from Enfield, but he'd already caught the look on my face.

"Oh, come now. You're jealous?" Enfield stood up and clapped my shoulder. "I'm sure it's nothing. Have you and Henry spoken at all? I think I've seen him only once or twice in the past several weeks."

"Letters. But lately his writings have become so strange. He doesn't sound like himself at all." I touched my pocket where the last letter I received from him was secreted.

Enfield nodded. "I'm sure we'll get it straightened out, but in the meantime you should try to put your mind elsewhere. I hate seeing you so upset. I'll see you tomorrow?"

"Yes. I plan to go see Henry myself to try to get everything sorted out." I supposed I'd answered my own question—I couldn't wait for Henry to come around. I would go seeking.

"I'll come with you," Enfield said.

When he'd left I took up his spot in the chair. I pulled the unopened letter from my pocket and held it in my palm, testing its weight. I did this every time one of his letters arrived. The heavy ones set my head spinning because they were sure to contain stories about his work with his father or his family or the time he took for himself in the park. He wondered if he might join me in the country one day, because London had become a drain on him in ways he could never seem to fully express.

But this letter was not heavy. Whatever it was, it was composed on a single sheet of paper. It would not contain stories of his day-to-day life now that he was no longer a student at the London School. He was with his father all the time now, and the thinness of it set me on edge. There should have been more to tell, not less.

I slipped my finger under the lip of the envelope and, as my heart beat wildly in my chest, opened it.

There was no greeting, no kind words.

This will be my last letter to you. This is over.

I am sorry, Gabriel, but you must try to understand. Look what my feelings for you have wrought. I was expelled, my father fired for simply trying to help me. And we cannot deny that we place ourselves in a precarious position by nature of our very existence.

What I know is that I cannot deny this part of me. It lives and breathes and so I have no choice but to excise that which is causing my heart to break. Maybe then, I can find a way to live with myself.

You said to me once that we deserve to live, Gabriel, and we do. You deserve a life free from this . . . this knowing. I used to think I did as well, but now I'm just not sure.

Do not look for me. Do not seek me out.

                                        Goodbye, Gabriel.

In the pit of my stomach there grew an ache that started as a smoldering ember, but quickly burned through every part of me like a raging inferno. The pain was unbearable.

I stood, letting the letter fall to the floor. My breaths came in short gasps. I didn't bother trying to keep my legs steady under me. I let them fold as I collapsed onto the floor. Bracing my hands against the wooden planks, trying to hold my world together.

My dearest Henry. What has happened to you?

———

I planned to go to Henry's as soon as I could. If I could see him, if I could speak to him, maybe I'd be able to get through to him. There must have been a reason for his change of heart. Something was causing him to doubt, and it must have been something new, or perhaps . . . *someone* new. The thought made my stomach turn over and I second-guessed myself—should I seek Henry out after he'd told me not to? Was he trying to keep me from learning something that would break me?

I had no appetite, so I skipped Miss Laurie's breakfast entirely and headed straight to Sir Carew's office on the far side of the London School's campus. He was already there, and because of the early hour, I assumed we would be alone together for a long while before his first patrons arrived. The thought set me on edge.

When I walked in, he glanced up at me. "You're in rather early, Utterson. I wasn't expecting you for another hour."

"Yes, sir. I thought I'd get a head start on my work."

"Very good of you," Sir Carew said. "Very good, indeed." His gaze swept over me, and I had to clench the lapels of my jacket to keep myself from shuddering.

I quickly settled into a desk Sir Carew had prepared for me. As he'd instructed, I familiarized myself with the way he ran his office and the tasks he had hired me to perform.

My desk was angled away from Sir Carew's, facing the wall, a partition partially blocking his view, but as I sat there, I could still feel his eyes on me.

I immediately got to work verifying citations in Sir Carew's latest cases and compiling his notes, organizing them inside a leather folio. I worked into the early afternoon, trying desperately to keep Henry and the words from his letter out of my mind.

"You're very good at that." Sir Carew was suddenly standing directly behind me, resting his hands on my shoulders. The weight of them was so much heavier than it needed to be. "You'll be of great service to me, Gabriel."

I bit the inside of my cheek as the ink from my pen pooled on the paper in front of me, leaving a black stain that bled through to the papers underneath. He let go and mumbled something under his breath as he shuffled back to his desk. The chair creaked under him as he sat down, and the sound of his shallow, wavering breaths filled my ears. After a moment, he cleared his throat, and I turned just enough to see that he was watching me the way a hawk watches a mouse.

"I've taken on several new cases and I will require you to be here much more often than we'd previously agreed to," he said suddenly. "I'm sure you understand."

I hesitated. I didn't want to be alone with him any longer than was absolutely necessary.

"I'm sure your father would be very disappointed to hear you'd refused an opportunity such as this being a young man of your . . . background."

He seemed to enjoy bringing up how much he was doing for me at every possible opportunity. He didn't want me to forget that I was there only because he allowed it. I knew there may have been others with the knowledge to work in his office, but that wasn't the issue. The real question was, did they have the stomach for it?

"Yes, sir," I said through gritted teeth. "I'd be honored to help as much as I possibly can."

"Splendid!" he said with a sickening enthusiasm. "You'll start your extended shifts this evening. We'll be burning the candle at both ends, you and I."

I wanted to vomit.

———

Sir Carew was, at times, in awe of my abilities, my attention to detail, my innate ability to understand the complex laws that govern the medical world. To him, I was a Black boy possessed of exceptional talent—a testament to my kind. If I was a testament to the abilities of my people, then he was surely a testament to his—an overinflated ego stoked by unchecked entitlement, undeserving of the accolades heaped upon him for his thinly veiled attempts at decency. He was a brute and I detested him more than I could say.

As the days passed, I learned more and more about the law, its interpretations, and how flexible it was depending on the amount of money Sir Carew's clients did or did not have. In my time alone with Sir Carew I also came to understand that men like him do not have a limit to their depravity.

One evening, when the sun set, Sir Carew relieved me of my duties and I made my way to the courtyard. The evening air was unseasonably crisp, and it burned my lungs as I breathed it in, trying desperately to get the smell of Sir Carew's rancid breath and cigar smoke out of my nose.

Other students were standing around, laughing and joking with one another. None of these former classmates acknowledged me save for one—Samuel. As soon as he spotted me he made a beeline straight through the grass. I turned away, but he caught me by the shoulder and spun me around.

"Utterson!" he bellowed, as if he'd ever been anything but an arrogant, self-entitled prick. His eyebrows arched up and he nudged me hard in the ribs. "How's the clerking going? Sir Carew seems to have taken a liking to you."

The way he said it seemed to imply some other meaning. I wanted to punch him in his round, pink face.

"Where's Jekyll?" Samuel asked, clamping his hands down on my shoulders. "Haven't seen him around since the end of last school year. Are the two of you still . . . close?"

I roughly shook his hands off me. "It's none of your business."

He looked thoughtful. "Maybe not. But I can think of some-one whose business it is."

I glared at him. "And who is that?"

"Him." Samuel raised his hand and pointed across the court-yard to a figure moving around the outside edge of the tree-lined square. He had the collar of his coat pulled up to his ears. I peered into the darkness just as he passed under a streetlamp.

My heart sputtered.

The white hair was noticeable even at a distance. It was the young man who'd trampled the girl in front of Henry's house.

"They call him Hyde," Samuel said. "Not sure who found out his name seeing as he never speaks to anyone, but every once in a while, we see him nosing about campus." He grinned. "I think he'd be interested to know what the state of affairs is between you and Jekyll."

"And why is that?"

Samuel narrowed his eyes at me and the corner of his mouth drew up. "Because he's been in and out of Jekyll's house at his leisure. Using the back door, of course. Keeping things secret. He's visiting your friend more than you ever did."

I took a step toward the white-haired young man, but Samuel moved to cut me off.

"Get out of my way," I said.

"What are you going to do? Chase after him?" He grinned wider, but not in a way that showed anything other than rueful contempt. "You and Jekyll aren't as *close* as you used to be, are you?"

I'd had enough. "You've hated me since I set foot on this campus," I said angrily.

Samuel shrugged. "I can't deny it."

"And yet you keep tabs on me and Jekyll? You seem to know quite a bit about me and him and our private business." I leaned toward him. "Why is that, Samuel?"

His face paled and I couldn't tell if he wanted to punch me or run away. I shoved past him and he rejoined his friends, but as they laughed and joked at my expense, his expression remained a mask of bewilderment. Perhaps I'd struck a nerve.

The young man Samuel had called Hyde had disappeared from the courtyard, and before I could stop myself I was running toward the last place I saw him.

I cut through the buildings and ducked down the narrow street that abuts the London School to the north. Hurried footsteps moved away from me in the darkness.

The alleyways were a tangle of narrow passageways, circulating through the city like veins through the human body. I rushed forward, skidding around the corner and into an even narrower side street. As I rounded the corner, I finally caught a glimpse of Hyde. He was shuffling along, a hitch in his step as if he was pained in some way. I wondered if he was still suffering from the injuries sustained in the altercation with those terrible men from the alleyway.

He stopped suddenly, turning to face me as if he knew I'd be there. His face was shrouded in shadow, his hair like a white-hot flame in the pitch-dark.

"Are you looking for me, Utterson?"

He knew me.

I tried to recall if Enfield had used my name as we tended to the girl.

I began to answer, but as that voice seeped into my head, I could not seem to form a coherent thought. His was the strangest voice I'd ever heard. It was at once hollow and strained, but resonant like the lowest note on a piano.

"You know me?" I asked, suddenly enraged. Had Henry told him about me and if so, why? Henry couldn't even stand to be honest with himself about his feelings for me, and yet he'd clearly told this boy something. "Come out of the dark and show yourself," I demanded.

"I could," the young man said. "But where is the fun in that?"

In the silence of the alleyway, the sounds of nighttime London faded away, and I heard nothing except for the measured breathing of this strange person. His movements mirrored mine as I stepped to the side, angling for a better view of him.

A dreadful emotion rolled over me like the thick London fog. This breathing, this foreboding presence—I knew it. It was familiar to me, but I could not place it. A shiver ran up my back and across my scalp.

"What are you playing at?" I shoved down the growing sense of panic.

Water trickled between the bricks on either side of the alleyway—and something brushed my ankle with a skittering of small feet. A calamitous bang sent my heart into my throat and I spun around, nearly tripping over my own feet. A mangy cat was chasing whatever rodent had slipped by me and upended a stack of crates.

I gathered myself and turned back to look at the man Samuel had called Hyde.

I found nothing but the gloom.

———

I thought of nothing but his face, even though it chilled me to the bone to recall it. Everything about him had unnerved me, and I questioned my reasoning for this. As much as I hated to admit when Enfield was right, he may have had a point when he spoke of jealousy. I felt its keen sting. Knowing Hyde was seeing Henry face-to-face when I had not been permitted to do so in months bothered me.

A haze enveloped me as I made my way through the streets the following morning. My breath puffed out of me in clouds of white smoke as I pressed my collar tightly against my neck.

When I arrived at Sir Carew's office, my small desk was already piled high with notes needing to be compiled, cases that needed to be researched. I got to work straight away and tried my hardest to ignore my employer.

The bell above the office door clanged in the early afternoon as a tall man wearing glasses and a gray suit walked in carrying a scuffed briefcase. Sir Carew went to him and shook his hand much too vigorously for the man's liking. He roughly removed his hand from Sir Carew's grasp and stepped back.

"It's good to see you, Mr. Guest," Sir Carew said. "You're looking well. I trust you have some good news?"

The man glanced at me and I quickly returned my gaze to the work at my desk.

"I suppose so," he said as he set his briefcase down and adjusted his glasses.

Sir Carew rubbed his hands together and returned to his seat. "All of this is quite pointless, I can assure you. I have no doubt that Mr. Hopkins is guilty of fraud."

"Will a court of law decide this man's fate based solely on your assurances?" Mr. Guest asked.

I gripped my pen and clenched my jaw, waiting for Sir Carew to snap at him, but he only huffed loudly.

"My life might be much easier if they would," Sir Carew said.

I angled my head just enough to see his desk out of the corner of my eye.

"It just so happens that your suspicions are correct this time."

Mr. Guest removed several papers from his case and set them down. "You suspected that Mr. Hopkins forged his employer's signature to secure a large personal loan shortly after his employer's unfortunate and untimely death. Mr. Hopkins denies it, of course, and says he simply waited a little longer than is customary to present his documents to the bank."

"How very convenient," Sir Carew grumbled.

"I studied the angle of the letters, the pressure of the pen, the type of ink." Mr. Guest's voice rose as he spoke as if the subject excited him. "The signatures are nearly identical."

Sir Carew leaned forward, his fingers tented under his chin. "Nearly?"

Mr. Guest reached out and traced his finger along the papers he had presented to Sir Carew. "Mr. Hopkins would have gotten away with this had it not been for me. He is very good but alas, he is a liar and a fraud. He forged the signature of his employer. There is, as you've said, no doubt."

Sir Carew clapped his hands together and quickly secured this new evidence in his desk. "He'll spend twenty years behind bars when I'm done with him. I'll see to it that his wife and children are left destitute."

The joy he took in punishing people made me ill. I turned away and tried to focus on my work as Mr. Guest left and Sir Carew partook in a glass of brandy and a celebratory cigar.

Nearly an hour later, Sir Carew approached my desk.

"Utterson," he said. "Take this letter to the secretary, Miss

Prinze, at the school's main office. Tell her to deliver it to Sir Hastings before day's end."

"Yes, sir," I said as he slipped the sealed letter into my hand. He gripped the letter tighter when I tried to take it. He smirked and finally let it go.

I was so grateful for a chance to get out of the stuffy office and away from Sir Carew that I rushed out without my coat. Even as the cold nipped at the skin of my neck and wrists, I decided not to go back to retrieve my jacket lest Sir Carew find something else for me to do in his odious presence.

I trudged across the courtyard and made my way to the front office, where Miss Prinze was busy composing letters behind her desk. She glanced up, her spectacles teetering on the tip of her nose.

"Mr. Utterson," she said warmly. "It's good to see your face."

"Yes, ma'am. I'm delivering a letter for Sir Carew. He asks that you make sure it's in Sir Hastings's hand by the end of the day today."

I handed her the letter and as she grasped it, she also took hold of my hand. Her bottom lip trembled as if she was on the verge of tears.

"Are you all right?" I asked.

She shook her head, looked around the empty office, and leaned close to me. "Sir Carew is a beastly man."

My heart sputtered in my chest. "Ma'am?"

Miss Prinze gripped my hand so tight it sent a bolt of pain

into my wrist. "I know you're working for him now." She lowered her voice further and narrowed her gaze so severely she almost looked like a different person. "A letter opener is quite an effective weapon, Mr. Utterson. If it's well maintained. Sharp."

I pulled my hand from hers. "I don't take your meaning, but I can assure you—"

"Forget I said anything," she said, tucking the letter into a stack of other sealed envelopes and resuming her work. "I'll see to it that your letter is delivered."

I turned to leave but paused at the door. "Sir Carew has a fine collection of letter openers."

Her gaze locked on mine. She nodded and we shared a moment of silent understanding.

Outside, my legs began to wobble, threatening to give out on me at any moment, so I steadied myself against the brick exterior of the building. Despite the chill, a thin film of sweat blanketed my brow. Miss Prinze knew Sir Carew was a brute. In her eyes was the same fear I saw in my own when I'd had occasion to look in a mirror—something I found harder and harder to do lately.

The chilly London air was bearable compared to the stifling atmosphere inside Sir Carew's office, compared to the air he blew through his rotting teeth onto the back of my neck as he lorded over me. I pressed the back of my head into the wall and shut my eyes for a moment, gathering my thoughts.

I decided that I hadn't seen the rear courtyard in a while and that now was the perfect time to revisit it. Anything to keep me from having to sit in that office any longer than was absolutely necessary.

I took the narrow stone path that led around the back of the main building. The grass was beginning to creep over the edges of the paving stones. The late afternoon hour had seen most of the students and faculty take their leave, and the rear courtyard was almost always empty at that time. But as I rounded the corner, someone was ascending the steps that led up from the basement of the main building.

I caught sight of him before he saw me, but even at a distance, even though I had not set eyes on him in months, I recognized Henry as surely as I'd recognize my own reflection.

I pressed my back against the building. There was no cover. No place for me to hide—though why that was the first thing I wanted to do was beyond me. I had dreamed of seeing Henry's face every second we'd been apart, and now that he was within shouting distance, I could not force myself to make a single sound. The words calling out to him were stuck in my throat, where they threatened to choke me as I took in Henry's appearance.

He was disheveled. His pants were unhemmed and frayed at the ankles, his coat sporting a hole in the sleeve. His hair was unkempt and the scruff of a week's worth of beard—a beard he used to be meticulous about shaving off every other day—was now thick enough to cover the lower half of his face, obscuring his mouth.

He didn't look up but instead focused intently on his work, which appeared to be awkwardly lugging a steamer trunk up the basement steps. A single horse and small cart awaited him on the narrow strip of carriage pathway. As he loaded the trunk onto it, he paused, tipped his head to the hazy sky, and sighed. A cloud of white smoke pushed out of him.

I stepped away from the building and raised my hand to wave at him. "Henry!"

His body went rigid. He angled his head toward me as I approached him but didn't turn to face me fully.

There was something about Henry's demeanor that was wholly unfamiliar. Had we been apart so long that he had become a different person to me? I thought for a moment that maybe I'd made a mistake. Perhaps this wasn't my Henry after all.

He pulled the collar of his jacket in close and mounted his horse in one quick motion. It was then that I saw his face. While there was no doubt that he was in fact my Henry, something terrible had happened. He was changed in a way I could not fully describe. The hollows under his normally bright eyes were cavernous. The eyes themselves were dull and glassy, like a doll's eyes. His skin was ashen and his lips were dry and cracked. I'd never seen him this way before.

"Henry," I said, taking a tentative step toward him. "Henry, I've been hoping—"

He spurred his horse and took off with such a calamitous uproar that it set my heart racing. The horse barreled directly toward me, Henry driving the animal forward with a frenzied look in his wild, terrified eyes. I dove out of the way just as it sped past and I tumbled into a patch of dying garden, cracking my knee against an errant stone.

Henry didn't so much as look back.

Soon I could no longer hear the pounding of the horse's hooves, only the beating—the breaking—of my own heart.

———

I returned to Sir Carew's office, Henry's wild eyes seared into my mind's eye. It was as if he hadn't seen me at all, as if I were a ghost to him.

Sir Carew drank himself into a stupor as the late afternoon faded and the evening rolled in. I was able to collect my jacket and slip out just as he rested his head on his desk and began to snore.

The light was gone from the sky by the time I reached Leicester Square. Henry's horse was tethered to a post in the alleyway, and the cart was parked next to it, still cradling the steamer trunk Henry had loaded into it.

I secreted myself in the shadows of the building directly across the street and waited. For what, I didn't know. Henry was not himself, and I needed to speak with him.

After nearly an hour, with my fingertips numb from the chilly nighttime air, a light broke in the alleyway. The rear door to the Jekyll residence opened and a hazy orange glow filtered out. A shadow moved into the alley and there was the sound of footfalls and grunting as the trunk was pulled from the cart. The scraping of the wood and steel across the ground cut through the night and rattled me.

I stepped from my hiding place and carefully crossed the street. Pressing myself against the corner wall, I peered around, holding my breath, preparing to take in the strange sight of Henry's appearance.

But as I caught a glimpse of the person in the alleyway, I was taken aback. It wasn't Henry at all, but Hyde.

He lugged the trunk across the threshold and closed the door behind him, plunging the alley into darkness.

Hyde.

The name stuck in my head and on my tongue. He was there at that very moment with Henry. *My* Henry—who now acted as if he could not see me though I was right in front of him.

I had not thought myself a jealous person, but Henry was avoiding me, writing me letters to tell me he could not see me, and yet Hyde was free to come and go? And my interactions with this odd young man had been stranger still. The slight was more than I could bear. If I could not get answers from Henry about the state of his mind or his feelings for me, I would seek to find out as much as I could about his strange new companion.

If he was Hyde, then I would be Seek.

CHAPTER 10

A Friend in Lanyon

I FOUND LANYON IN THE COURTYARD OF HIS FAMILY'S HOME IN Cavendish Square the following morning. The manor was big enough to fit three of Miss Laurie's boardinghouses comfortably in its footprint. Lanyon had never been boastful about his circumstances, but I wouldn't have blamed him if he had been.

"Gabriel?" he asked as he left his younger sisters to their tea party and met me at the front gate. "What are you doing here?"

"I don't mean to impose," I said.

"Of course not," he said, opening the gate and ushering me inside. "Forgive me, Gabriel. I haven't had a friend visit in quite some time."

"Because you have no friends," his youngest sister said with a giggle. She was nearly invisible in her tangle of ruffled skirts and perfectly pinned ringlets.

"Gabriel, this is Emma," Lanyon said, pointing to the girl who looked to be about six. "And this is Audre." The other girl's feet dangled above the ground as she teetered on the edge of her chair. She couldn't be older than four.

"Will you be joining us for tea?" Emma asked. "My brother is very rude for not inviting you."

Lanyon laughed. "In my defense, you two sprung this impromptu gathering on me. If I'd have known, I would have avoided the garden altogether."

Audre slid off her chair and slipped her little hand into mine.

"Is he very rude to you? I will tell Mother." She patted my hand and returned to her seat as Lanyon threw his hands up in defeat.

"My own flesh and blood would throw me to the wolves?" He pretended to be wounded, shaking his head and clutching his chest. "Come, Gabriel. Let us leave these traitors to their tea."

The girls giggled and clinked the rims of the cups together as Lanyon ushered me to a bench in a secluded part of the garden. Vines of lavender wisteria climbed an ivory latticework and shielded us from prying eyes.

"I'm glad you've come," Lanyon said. "I've missed receiving your letters, but since you're here in the flesh, well . . ." He trailed off.

Lanyon had written to me during my time away, expressing concern for me and for Henry. I had assured him there was nothing to be concerned about, but that wasn't true anymore. Our letters had gone from curious concern to the friendliest of exchanges, and I counted him among my friends.

"I heard on campus you're now working for Sir Carew? Why didn't you tell me?"

"It's something I'd like to forget," I said honestly.

Lanyon pursed his lips and ran his hand through his shock of chestnut-brown curls. "I see."

"That's what I've come to speak to you about."

"Of course. What can I do?"

I sighed. "I'm not sure where to begin. You've heard the rumors about me, but have you heard what happened to Henry?"

Lanyon narrowed his eyes at me. "I have. Though the accounts are sure to have been . . . overembellished. They say he's holed up in his father's laboratory."

"I think that's true," I said, nodding. "Have you seen him?"

"Recently?" Lanyon's brows pushed together. "No. Why?"

"We kept up our correspondence over the summer, but his last letter—" I swallowed the sadness as it crept up my throat. "Things have been complicated between us. Now he refuses to see me. By chance, I saw him yesterday on campus. I called out to him and he acted as if I were invisible. I know he heard me calling to him. I stood in the road like some damned fool thinking he'd stop, but he nearly killed me with his cart."

Lanyon's jaw fell open. "Gabriel . . . you can't be serious. I can't imagine Henry ever doing something like that to you. Are you certain he saw you?"

I nodded and Lanyon sighed. "The two of you have always been very close," he said.

I exchanged a knowing glance with him. "And now, there's this other boy," I continued.

"Who?" Lanyon asked.

"His name is Hyde. I've seen him coming and going from Henry's house at all hours. I have only had a few encounters with him, but they've each been . . . strange."

"What do you mean?" asked Lanyon.

I shrugged and leaned back against the bench. "I don't know how to explain it. It's as if he is taunting me."

"Why would he—" He stopped short. "Gabriel, if Henry has taken a liking to another student—"

"He's not a student," I said. "At least I don't think he is, and I don't think Henry and he are . . . well . . . I don't know what they are, but regardless, why would he treat me this way? I've never done anything except—" I had to stop and gather myself. Tears threatened to overflow, and I tipped my head back. "I've never done anything except be there for him, and I thought he felt the same. I thought he would always be here for me when I needed him."

Lanyon put his hand on my shoulder. "First loves are a fickle thing, my friend. After the sweet there is often the sour, and it leaves a bitter taste."

I didn't want to think of it that way, but Lanyon had a point. Is that what had become of us? We'd simply grown apart and this was the inevitable outcome of Henry moving on?

I stood, shoving my hands in my pockets. "No," I said angrily. "No, that's not it. I'd want him happy under any circumstance. This is not that. There's some relationship there, yes. But the nature of it is still in question."

"Okay, Gabriel," Lanyon said, patting the air in front of him. "I believe you, but what can be done?"

I considered lying to him. My gut was telling me that something was terribly amiss, and I wasn't sure I wanted to involve him more than I already had. I also considered how Lanyon might see me and what judgment he would hold—of my chasing around after Henry, after this boy Hyde.

Lanyon seemed to sense my hesitation to elaborate on my plan. He stood and came to my side, placing his hand on my shoulder again. "Trust me, my friend. Whatever you're planning to do, please know that I enjoy all sorts of nearly nefarious activities."

"Nearly nefarious?" I asked. "Do I even want to know what that means?"

He shook his head and laughed. "It's nothing so serious as to warrant that look in your eyes. Horses, mostly. If my mother knew about my betting habit, she might lock up my register."

I chuckled and gave Lanyon's arm a squeeze. "I intend to find out who this Hyde character is, where he comes from, and what the nature of his relationship with Henry is."

"And when you learn these things, what will you do?" Lanyon asked. "When you find that Henry has moved on, will you do the same?"

I didn't have an answer for him. I hadn't thought that far ahead. What I knew was that I needed answers, even if that meant learning that Henry and I would be parted for good.

CHAPTER 11

A Confrontation with the Man They Call Hyde

SIR CAREW DOUBLED MY WORKLOAD AND KEPT ME IN HIS SIGHTS AT nearly every waking moment. I was only able to put my plan into practice after a full week, and I feared I may have missed my chance. I didn't know it was possible to detest Sir Carew more than I already did, but as it turned out, there was no cup my hatred of him could not fill.

I wrote a letter and sent it to Henry's home, only for it to be returned to Miss Laurie's boardinghouse days later, unopened.

On an afternoon when Sir Carew fell ill and took to his bed, I was given a reprieve and used it to walk the streets surrounding Leicester Square. I saw Dr. Jekyll many times, coming and going from the family home sometimes by carriage, sometimes on foot. It occurred to me that my behavior was obsessive, maybe even inappropriate. I told myself that if I could catch a glimpse of Henry, if I could see him smiling, that

I would leave him to the choices he'd made, regardless of how my heart ached.

When I finally saw Henry emerge from the front door of his residence, trailing behind his father, his woolen coat pulled up around his neck, my heart leapt into a furious rhythm. But my excitement quickly turned to anguish as I took in Henry's sad state.

Even under the many layers of his clothing he was thinner than I had ever seen him. His face was gaunt, his eyes downcast. It took everything in me not to call out to him as I stepped from my hidden spot in the alleyway. He climbed into the carriage and it disappeared into the gloaming, and I was left standing alone in the street, unable to breathe.

————

Sir Carew was, much to my delight, still incapacitated the following day, and so I again made my way to Leicester Square in the early hours of the dim evening. A patchy fog had settled in, and as I stood like a sentry in the dark, a light went on in the room I knew to be Henry's. His bedroom was on the second floor, his window overlooking the street below. I pressed my back against the damp brick and held my breath as a figure moved to the window. The silhouette was familiar to me. Henry. He was so close and all I wanted was to see his face.

The curtains drew back and I braced myself, preparing to see

Henry's gaunt face. But instead I was met with a pair of shining eyes, a shock of white hair—

Hyde.

A wave of nausea swept me up like the tide to thrash me against the rocks. I staggered back. Hyde was in Henry's bedroom. Lanyon must have been right.

I leaned forward, resting my hands on my knees. This was what I'd been searching for—answers to an unending avalanche of questions. I had them now, and I hated myself for seeking them out in the first place. Henry's letters should have been enough.

I was a fool.

I turned to leave when across the road in the alleyway immediately next to Henry's home, the rear door opened. I glanced back up at the window to find Hyde gone and the light put out. As I leveled my eyes, dappled candlelight from the open door illuminated the alley, and a figure emerged from the gloom like a ghost. My heart beat against my ribs like a bird trying desperately to escape its cage.

Hyde strode across the street, his gait wide and just a bit off-balance. He stopped a few paces from me, and his wide dark eyes found me in the bleak night fog.

"Good evening," he said, his voice low and hollow.

I didn't know what to say. The heat of embarrassment rose in my face, and a heavy cloak of shame wrapped itself around me. I shouldn't have been there. I should have respected Henry's wishes. Now, I was crouching in the alley like the fool I was. I let my gaze wander to the ground.

"I'm sorry," I said. "I know I shouldn't be here."

"Where else should you be?" Hyde asked, stepping closer.

I lifted my head to meet his eyes. I expected to find anger there, perhaps even resentment, but I found something oddly comforting in his gaze.

"I've been trying to see Henry for some time," I said.

He studied my face in silence for several moments. "He wrote to you."

My heart cartwheeled in my chest. "He told you that?"

Hyde tilted his head. "He didn't have to. I know him very well. It seems like the kind of thing he would do. He asked you to forget him, didn't he?"

A carriage rumbled past and cloaked the already shadowy alleyway in total darkness. For a moment I was alone in the gloom with this strange young man, and I thought I saw his cheek lift, like he was smiling. The carriage moved on down the street, and the dim light filtering through the dense fog illuminated the alleyway once more.

Hyde was another step closer to me. I hadn't heard him move.

The hair at the nape of my neck lifted, and a cold sweat slicked my palms. "You—you know Henry well, then?"

"Better than he knows himself," Hyde said.

I huffed, feeling the green envy slip under my tongue and

color my words. "How is that possible? You haven't known him long enough."

"Oh, I know him. And I know he can't see past his own fear."

I was about to question him further when Hyde suddenly glanced down the alley. "You were here when those men were chasing me," he said in a voice that sounded like the rustle of leaves caught in the wind.

I'd nearly forgotten the trampling incident. "Yes. Why were they after you?"

Hyde rose his hands high over his head and spun in a circle, then bowed low, pretending to tip a hat he wasn't wearing.

I didn't know if I should laugh or run.

"I was in Hyde Park. It was my very first time there." He paused and gave another little spin. "The trees and the grass and my god—even the birds and the insects. Everything was alive and shifting and I—I love to dance."

I tried to hide how utterly confused I was. "What does that have to do with the men who were chasing you?"

"I love to dance," Hyde repeated. "They, apparently, do not."

There was something in his words that he was trying to convey, some other meaning that wasn't entirely clear. He watched me intently, his gaze so piercing I had to look away.

"I don't know how long I was out there," he said, rubbing his arms as if the chill was starting to get to him. "Those men saw me and told me to stop acting like a fool. They seemed to take my happiness as some terrible offense."

"Do you know them?"

"No," he said.

I was still confused. "They were running after you like you'd committed a crime."

Hyde huffed, and a cloud of white steam rippled out of him and mingled with the fog. "They treated me as if I'd been tried and convicted. They tried to accost me. None of them could move fast enough to catch me."

Hyde suddenly took hold of my arms. His grip was terribly strong. "I walked away, but when my back was turned, they fell on me. Tweaked my leg, split my lip open, injured my eye. I ran. There is no shame in running." He turned me around. "I think if you and your cousin Enfield had not been there, the punishment they would have liked to subject me to would have been far more severe. I suppose I have you to thank for that?"

Hyde was quite unlike anyone I'd ever met in my entire life. I could not pick apart what it was that made me feel this way. His prematurely gray-white hair was peculiar, but aside from that he didn't look any different than anyone else I might have passed on the street. I searched his face for some mark or sign that would tell me why I couldn't seem to look away from him, but found nothing.

"I'm well aware of the law," I said, turning my attention back to the matter at hand. "And dancing in Hyde Park isn't in violation of any of them, as far as I'm aware."

"You're well versed in the law?"

I stood a little straighter. "I am. I clerk for Sir Danvers Carew."

Hyde stiffened. His reaction to the name was familiar to me.

"You know him?" I asked.

"No," Hyde said, casting his gaze to the ground. "But I've heard of him, and not because he's some pious vulture of the law. He has quite a reputation in the dark."

I didn't know where Hyde had been spending his time since arriving in the company of the Jekylls, but the description did seem to fit Sir Carew. I shuddered. I knew what was said about him in the light—that he was brilliant, merciless in court, and dogged in his pursuit of young men whom he could manipulate. I could only imagine what was said about him *in the dark*.

Hyde approached me and leaned in so close I could feel his breath in my face.

"You're very close to Henry."

I peered into his face in the growing darkness. His large brown eyes were familiar and strange all at once.

"He is dear to me," I said. "It's why I'm here. I've seen you coming and going, and it made me question the nature of your relationship with him." I stopped myself from saying any more. I wanted to scream at him that it was killing me to see him so well received while I had been cast aside, forced to sulk in darkened, rat-infested alleyways, hoping to catch a mere glimpse of Henry. But I reminded myself of the promise I'd made—if this was what Henry wanted, I would accept it.

"I should not have come," I said, feeling thoroughly defeated. "Please don't tell Henry I was here. I'm embarrassed enough as it is."

"I don't think you have anything to be embarrassed about," Hyde said. "You've come after the boy you love to try to assess the state of his heart. How could you or he find anything about that embarrassing?"

I was so completely awestruck by the ease with which he spoke about me and Henry. There was no hint of malice or jealously, no sense of judgment.

"As far as not informing Henry that you've been here, well, I'm afraid I don't have a choice in that matter. I share everything with Henry."

"Please." Desperation grabbed hold of me. "He can't know I was here."

"Why?" asked Hyde. "Why can you not be honest with him? It's clear that the two of you have left things unsaid for far too long."

"He won't see me," I said. "You can't understand."

"Oh no?" Hyde asked. "You might be surprised."

I shook my head; it wasn't as simple as that. But I decided that if Hyde was going to say something to Henry, I couldn't stop him. There was no sense in trying.

I turned and brushed passed Hyde, making my way out into the street.

I paused, glancing behind me. "If you tell him I was here, at least do me the courtesy of also telling him that I only wish to see him happy." I turned away from him and stared into the fog.

Hyde's footsteps approached me from behind, but I dared not face him; I didn't want him to see the tears welling in my eyes. But I could hear his breaths coming in short, quick bursts.

And then suddenly his trembling hand was on my shoulder.

Let him see me at my worst, I thought. *Let him see everything.*

It didn't matter. Whether he was close to Henry or not made no difference. He was a stranger to me. I turned to face him, and as I did he quickly stepped behind me. In the confusion of our switching places I lost sight of him and then heard his footsteps hurrying across the road and into the alley abutting the Jekyll residence. His coat collar was pulled up so far it obscured his face. He entered the rear door and slammed it shut, cutting off the dappled light and plunging the alley into gloom.

I merely stood there for a moment, as if my feet were cemented to the ground, rattled by his abrupt departure. The heaviness of a new sadness pinned me to that place, even when I wanted nothing more than to leave.

Finally I forced myself away from the house. At the end of the street, I turned to look back at Henry's window only to find it dark. Empty.

CHAPTER 12

The Crooked House in Harrington

I saw Hyde's face in my dreams every night for a week. He was always lurking in the shadows or in some alleyway when I came upon him. He would see me watching him and burst forth, spinning and twirling like a puppet on a string.

I share everything with Henry.

I'd yell and scream that he needed to tell Henry that I wanted to speak with him, and he'd refuse and continue his dance.

I woke in a sweat, shivering until my bones ached.

Sir Carew recovered from his illness, much to my dismay. I knew my mother would tell me that it was wrong to wish ill on another man, but she didn't know him. I returned to work but I continued to hope for his worst health, his most bitter defeat.

Henry and Hyde consumed my thoughts even in my waking hours. I couldn't admit it to anyone except Lanyon and Enfield, who both implied that it was jealousy getting the better of me. Maybe they were right, but I felt that it was more than that. Hyde had not seemed confrontational so much as curious. He hadn't questioned my feelings for Henry at all. It was a welcome, if unnerving, response. Despite his seemingly innocent nature, I could not let it go. But I decided not to make it Henry's problem.

I stayed away from Leicester Square for a full week; when I found myself turning toward Henry's street as I walked to and from Sir Carew's office, I corrected course and went about my business.

One afternoon, as Miss Laurie was seeing off a group of her guests, she pulled me aside and asked if I'd go to Harrington's Market to bring her the freshly butchered hog she'd arranged for. I agreed, knowing that if I didn't, I'd just be wrestling myself away from Henry's street anyway. I could almost hear Enfield's voice in my head telling me to stop making such a fool of myself.

Harrington's was near the docks, tucked among warehouses and shipyards that dotted the River Thames. It stuck out like a festering sore. I could smell it before I saw it and when I finally came upon it, I had to hold my sleeve against my nose. I was thankful it wasn't yet summer—the smell would have been unbearable.

I pushed through the crowded stalls until I spotted my destination—a narrow building wedged between two others. A small shop with wide glass windows was situated on the ground floor. As I ducked inside I was grateful for the reprieve from the stink outside.

Cured meats and links of sausage hung from hooks in the low ceiling. Arranged on a wooden counter were other cuts of animals I didn't recognize immediately. The shop smelled of wood and smoke and salt. A burly man with a neatly trimmed beard and one eye clouded milky white stood behind the counter.

"Miss Laurie sent me to pick up a hog," I said.

The man's expression softened immediately and he leaned forward on the counter. "Oh right. She told me you'd be stopping by. I was hoping she might change her mind and make the trip herself. A fine woman, that Miss Laurie."

"She is," I said, though I understood he didn't mean it in the same way that I did. Miss Laurie had become something like a mother to me. I thought this man might fancy her as a wife. Little did he know that Miss Laurie spoke often of how she would never take a husband because she simply didn't want some man living in her house and eating her food.

"I've almost got everything ready." He looked me over, then glanced outside. "You sure you'll be able to manage it? You didn't bring a cart?"

"I can manage," I said.

He shrugged and disappeared down a narrow stairway at the back of the shop. I was busying myself, trying to guess which meaty bits belonged to which animals, when a familiar face bobbed past the window.

Hyde. Who was shortly followed by the Jekylls' butler, Mr. Poole.

I was tripping out the door before I could stop myself, all of my self-control out the window. Hyde leaned on a cane as he kept pace ahead of Mr. Poole. He vanished around the corner as Mr. Poole shouted something at him, but I couldn't make it out in the crush of voices.

I started after them at once, abandoning the butcher shop. Mr. Poole followed Hyde around the corner and I in turn followed him, keeping as much of a distance as I could manage without losing them entirely.

We zigzagged through the stalls and cramped alleyways until we were in a section of the dockside market I didn't recognize. There were far fewer people there, and by the time Hyde slowed his pace, I had to duck behind a stack of crates to avoid being seen.

"I can't keep up!" Mr. Poole said angrily, sweat beading on his brow, chest heaving.

Hyde gave the cane a little twirl and tapped it on the ground. "You're spry as ever."

Had he known the Jekyll family so long? Henry had never once mentioned him and yet he seemed to be intimately aware of the littlest details. A wave of annoyance rolled over me.

"But we're here, so you can rest," Hyde said. "I'll only be a moment."

"Oh no," Mr. Poole said, stomping up to him. "Dr. Jekyll said I was not to leave your side for a single second. And do you know what I find very funny?"

Hyde rolled his eyes and then leveled them at Mr. Poole. "Do tell."

"You've been high-stepping from the very moment we left the carriage. You don't even need that cane."

Hyde tossed the cane up and caught it again, then pointed it at Mr. Poole. "My knee is still tweaked from my little encounter with that ravenous pack of dolts chasing me and making me injure that poor child."

I was surprised to learn that he did seem to feel some remorse for what had happened.

"All of that aside," said Mr. Poole. "If I didn't know better, I'd say you were trying to lose me on purpose."

"And why would I want to do that?" Hyde asked.

"Because you don't really want to help poor Henry."

Hearing Henry's name created in me the most familiar ache. I missed him, and I felt it in my bones.

Hyde shifted his grip on the cane, looming over Mr. Poole. I realized then that its handle was shaped like an eagle's head. The glinting ruby eyes caught the light.

Dr. Jekyll's cane.

Hyde gripped the walking stick. "The *only* thing I want to do is help Henry. Same as Dr. Jekyll."

"Are you sure about that?" Mr. Poole asked. "Call me cynical but I don't think that's what you want at all."

Hyde huffed and stepped around him. "Stay here."

Hyde turned and went to a narrow door in one of the

buildings. He knocked three times and a moment later, a stout older woman in a black dress opened the door. Hyde disappeared inside, leaving Mr. Poole alone.

I crouched lower, my heart racing. The way Mr. Poole had said Henry's name—it was as if he pitied him. And Hyde's insistence that all he wanted to do was help seemed out of place. Henry could have confided in me about anything. I would have listened and tried to help in any way I could. I wasn't sure I believed Hyde when he said he wanted to help Henry, but I hoped it was true. I gathered myself and stepped from behind the stack of crates.

Mr. Poole's eyes widened. "Mr. Utterson? What on earth are you doing here?"

I glanced toward the door. The last thing I needed was for Hyde to go off and tell Henry he'd had another run-in with me.

"I came to see about a hog for Miss Laurie," I said. "I saw you and Hyde go by the window and—"

"You should not be here," Mr. Poole said suddenly. He rushed forward and tried to usher me back down the narrow alleyway. "You need to leave this instant."

"Mr. Poole, please," I said, planting my feet firmly. "Is something wrong with Henry? I'm sorry, but I overheard some of your conversation and I'm worried."

"It's nothing to worry about." Mr. Poole was a terrible liar. He glanced over his shoulder at the door Hyde had disappeared behind, then sighed and hung his head. "I saw you speaking with Hyde the other night outside the Jekyll residence."

The weight of embarrassment nearly folded me in half. "I—I'm sorry. I didn't want to intrude but—"

"You should cease all communication with him at once," Mr. Poole said flatly. "You have no idea what is happening and if I'm being honest, neither do I."

Something in him broke. His shoulders rolled forward and for a moment I thought he might faint. I put my hands on his shoulders to steady him and he grasped my wrist.

"This is the first time I've been asked to go with Hyde on this errand," Mr. Poole whispered. "This task has been previously handled by Dr. Jekyll himself or Henry. But now Henry is holed up in the lab with his father and they toil day and night. The only one permitted to enter at his leisure is Hyde. I have been in the paid service of the Jekylls for twenty years, and now they task this strange young man with important errands. Dr. Jekyll and Henry trust him implicitly." He stopped himself and cupped his wrinkled hands over his mouth. "I've said far too much. Please do not breathe a word of what I've shared with you to anyone. I beg of you."

"I won't," I said. I pitied the man; whatever was going on, he seemed very upset by it. "But I don't understand. Hyde speaks as if he is the one closest to Henry. He is comfortable enough to go in and out of their residence, their lab, as he pleases—"

Mr. Poole nodded. "You find it strange and you should. It is! This is madness and I am afraid, Mr. Utterson. Afraid!"

I didn't know Mr. Poole well enough to know if he was prone to exaggeration. My interactions with him had been mostly formal, but he seemed levelheaded. As he stood in front of me I saw a man stricken to his core by some terror he could not fully express.

There came the sound of heavy footsteps, and Mr. Poole shooed me away. I scampered behind the crates just as Hyde reemerged from the building carrying a small parcel wrapped in brown paper tied with string.

"Keep up, Mr. Poole," Hyde said as he sauntered down the street in the opposite direction, away from my hiding spot.

Mr. Poole did as he was told, and I waited until they were out of sight to leave my perch. I knew Miss Laurie was waiting for me to deliver her hog, and so I made note of the location of the crooked little house and returned to the butcher shop. As I wove through the maze of interconnected streets, my mind ran in circles.

I didn't know if I'd be able to keep the promise I'd made to myself—to give Henry the space he needed. Mr. Poole's demeanor had made me fear for Henry's safety.

———

I lugged the hog back to Miss Laurie's. She laughed as I set it down on the table.

"It's nearly as big as you are," she said. "And how is Mr. Loft?"

I raised an eyebrow. "He's well," I said. "He was hoping you'd come to get the hog yourself."

She waved her hands in the air. "Can you imagine me carrying that thing from there to here? I'd be laid up for a week. If he was any sort of gentleman, he'd have delivered it."

"I don't know if he was a gentleman or not, but I know I smell like an outhouse."

She pinched her nose. "Go get that stink off you." As I made my way upstairs she called after me. "A letter arrived for you. I stuck it under your door."

Suddenly the odor of rotting meat and congealed blood that clung to me wasn't such a pressing issue. I stumbled up the last few steps and raced to my room. On the floor was a letter with my name scrawled across the front in Henry's hand.

Meet me tomorrow night at 183 Dorset Street, Christ Church. Come alone.

I pressed the letter to my chest. Tomorrow night could not come soon enough.

CHAPTER 13

Sir Danvers Carew, Monster

I WENT TO SIR CAREW'S OFFICE THE NEXT DAY AS IF I WERE FLYING on invisible wings. Seeing Henry's letter had set me at ease and given me something to hope for, to look forward to. I would see him and, more importantly, I would get to see him because that's what he wanted. *He* was calling on *me* after all this time.

I kept the letter secreted in my pocket and touched it between the monotonous work of transcribing Sir Carew's nearly indecipherable handwriting. It was a welcome reminder that there was an entire world outside of Sir Carew's office, far from his prying eyes.

As I watched the hours tick by, Sir Carew became increasingly agitated. His restless nature was not new to me. On a near weekly basis, there came a point that he would become so flustered that he would purposely rock back on his chair, causing it to creak loudly. He would tap his fingers against the wooden desk and clear his throat over and over again.

The point of all of this was to capture my attention. He wanted me to turn and look at him. I'd learned early on that acknowledging him when he behaved this way fueled some strange mechanism in him. It was like a game, and if I looked up, he won. He would proceed to approach me and say all manner of deplorable things simply because he took my forced acknowledgment of him as a sign that I wanted him to interact with me in this way. Nothing could have been further from the truth.

Sir Carew began to hum an unfamiliar tune. When that didn't work in drawing my attention, he began to cough. I didn't look up, but I did hope with every fiber of my being that he would choke to death right there at his desk.

"Utterson," he said finally. "Are you quite all right?"

I clenched my jaw. He asked the question knowing full well the problem did not lie with me.

"I don't know what you mean, sir," I said without making eye contact. "I should be asking you if you're all right. You've been very ill and that cough sounds . . . concerning."

I hadn't asked him about his ill health because I didn't care, but clearly he'd noticed and now he had something to say about it.

"After everything I've done for you," he said as he approached me. "After everything I've given you, you haven't been concerned about my health until this very moment?"

He clamped his hands down on my shoulders. My inkpot tipped over, the black liquid spilling across a page of Sir Carew's notes. I braced myself for the onslaught of yelling and cursing, but he said nothing.

Then he leaned down and put his mouth close to my ear. "You owe me your life, boy. Never forget that."

I gripped the pen so hard it splintered. The sound of his heavy breathing, the smell of his breath—it sent a wave of nausea straight through me.

"Stand up," Sir Carew said.

"Sir, I've got so much work to do." My heart crashed in my chest. "I can have all of this done for you by morning if you would just permit me to concentrate."

Sir Carew huffed and squeezed my shoulder so hard I wanted to cry out. But I did not, for fear this reaction would only stoke whatever terrible flame burned within him. I set my broken pen down, stood up, and turned to face him. I felt like I couldn't breathe, couldn't move.

Sir Carew stared into my eyes. "Does your father know about you?" he asked.

I swallowed the fear that threatened to rise up my throat and ring out. "I—I don't know what you mean."

Sir Carew pushed closer until his stomach was pressing against mine. He smiled a wicked, twisted grin, then laughed, and his brandy-soaked breath invaded my nostrils. He placed his hand on my chest and let it trail down the front of me until his fingers brushed the waist of my trousers.

I reacted before I could think it through. I smacked his hand away from me and backed up until I was half perched on the edge of my desk.

The look of utter shock on his face was satisfying, but that little glimmer of retribution was quickly overtaken by fear. This man was used to getting what he wanted. He'd probably never been told no in his entire pathetic life and there I was, handing him this first defeat.

He picked up my candle, which had burned almost to the socket of the heavy brass candlestick, and brought it across the side of my head with one swift blow.

Everything went black. I tipped straight off the desk and hit the floor. I couldn't see anything, but I could hear Sir Carew screaming incoherently at the top of his lungs.

I felt the floorboards under my hands and under the right side of my face. I tried to blink away the darkness. Sir Carew's yelling let me know I was still alive, but as the pain flooded in I almost wished I wasn't. Agony bloomed in my temple and traced a path to the flesh around my eye.

I rolled onto my back and blinked until the beams criss-crossing the ceiling came into focus—and along with them Sir Carew's angry, twisted face. His pale skin was flushed pink. The wispy hair that normally lay over his head like a threadbare blanket was plastered to his sweaty brow. His eyes burned with the kind of hatred I'd seen a million times. It was the anger that screamed *How dare you defy me.*

Sir Carew's hands were suddenly on me, pulling me roughly to my feet. He clutched my collar so tight I couldn't breathe. I clawed at his hands.

"Look what you've done!" he shouted. "Blood all over my floor! Ink all over my papers!"

I glanced at the floor where my blood was indeed spilled across the wooden planks, though how any of that was my fault was beyond me. I pressed my hand to the side of my head to try to stem the trickle of warmth trailing down my face. As I did, my fingers sank into a deep gash over my right eye. The world began to shrink as the socket pulsed and the skin swelled.

Sir Carew shoved me toward the door. "This is over for you! Go run to your slum and make sure to write your father and tell him what a disgusting disappointment you are!"

He gave me a final shove, and I stumbled out into the courtyard. Few students were out at that time of night, but the ones that were didn't stop to help me as I struggled to find my footing. I collapsed onto the cold paving stones and didn't even attempt to get up.

Sir Carew stood in the doorway of his office, glaring down at me. "Stay down there in the dirt, Gabriel. It is where your kind belong. Trust me, boy—when all is said and done, you won't be able to show your face anywhere under the Queen's watchful eye. Mark my words."

He slammed the door and drew the curtains.

I lay against the cool ground, looking up at a scattering of twinkling stars. Perhaps it was all over for me—my clerking position gone would mean I'd need to leave Miss Laurie's. She'd offered to allow me to stay regardless, but how could I? The kind of ire I'd provoked in Sir Carew was sure to have some consequence; I couldn't allow Miss Laurie to get caught up in that. Leaving Miss Laurie's meant I'd have to return home. I'd have to leave Henry.

Henry.

I pulled my coat in close and took his letter from my pocket. The address was in Christ Church, which meant a long, terrible walk. But it didn't matter. I needed to get there, and so I gathered myself up and began my journey.

CHAPTER 14

A Room in Christ Church

I HITCHED A RIDE WITH A MERCHANT WHO, SEEING MY WOUND, offered me the bed of his cart. I gladly took it, lying among the sheepskins and tanned hides, fading in and out of either sleep or unconsciousness—I wasn't sure which. The cart suddenly stopped.

"This is as far as I'm going in this direction," said the merchant. "You'd best be off. And have someone fix that cut up before it goes bad."

I thanked him and made my way to 183 Dorset Street. The tenement was in worse shape than Miss Laurie's boardinghouse, something I hadn't believed was possible. All the rotted buildings on the street had a sinister way of sloping into the darkened alleyways below.

A woman carrying a screaming, dirty child smiled through her broken teeth at a man who waved a check register in her face and wetted his lips to offer her a kiss. A group of men fell drunkenly over themselves as they exited a pub singing some unfamiliar tune and shouting vulgar things at the women wandering the streets.

The streets surrounding Miss Laurie's smelled of animal waste, boiled food, and smoke. There on Dorset Street it seemed they were in short supply of food and fire but had an overabundance of waste, human and animal alike.

I rechecked the address, and when I was sure it was correct, I went to the door numbered 183 and knocked. A moment later a tall, striking woman pulled it open and looked me up and down. She wore a floor-length green dress with lacy bell-shaped sleeves and a plunging neckline. Her hair was folded into an elaborate roll that ran up the back of her head and was accented with little sprigs of tiny white flowers.

"Looks like you've had your ass handed to you, love." Her voice was raspy and thick with phlegm. She coughed into a yellowed lace handkerchief and then shoved her hand down on her hip. "Can I be of some service to you?"

"I'm looking for someone. Henry Jekyll? He gave me this address."

"Jekyll?" She looked thoughtful. "No Jekyll here, love."

There was suddenly a pounding of footsteps on the stairs, and a familiar face appeared at her shoulder.

Hyde.

"It's for me," he said. But when his eyes met mine, his face went blank. He took in my wounds in one sweeping glance and something flickered in his eyes. I thought it might have been anger, but he had no reason to care about my broken face.

"Come in," Hyde said.

Before I could protest, he grabbed my arm and pulled me inside. The woman in the green dress shut the door and turned at least three locks.

The entryway led to two small rooms on either side of a short hallway, at the end of which was a set of stairs. A half dozen women lounged about on various pieces of mismatched furniture. Some of them weren't women at all but girls, some as young as maybe ten.

There was another knock at the door, and a hush fell over the place.

"I know you're in there, Helena!" a man's voice called. "Open up and let me get a look at your pretty face."

The woman who'd opened the door reached inside her skirts and produced a small, glinting blade. She turned it over in her hands as she went to the door and opened it just enough to stick her arm out and put the blade under the man's chin.

"I'll say this but one time, Mr. Delaney, so listen well and do not take me for a game, because I know every move, every cheat. Understand?"

"Helena," the man protested.

She pressed the knife against his throat. From my time at the London School, I knew her blade hovered just over his carotid artery. If she cut him there, he'd be dead just as soon as he hit the ground.

"I have no need or want of your presence," Helena said, her tone stern and utterly uncompromising. "And if you show your face around here ever again, I will slice it off and wear it as a mask at my next masquerade celebration. Are we clear?"

The man stumbled back, and Helena shut the door, locking it up tight again. A young girl maybe a year younger than me ran up and embraced her.

"Don't you worry, Helena," said the girl. "If he comes around again, I'll kill him dead."

I'd had some assumption of what that place was when I saw how many young women were sheltered there. Houses of ill repute were well-known in Christ Church, but this place was something else. Helena seemed to be sheltering a coven of young women who were prepared to put men like the very unfortunate Mr. Delaney in the ground. With the images of Sir Carew still fresh in my mind, I could find no fault in their actions.

I turned to Hyde, who motioned for me to follow him upstairs.

I trailed him down a hallway and we entered a small room at the back of the house. There was a bed and two chairs, a small hearth, and a basin filled with water. I sank into one of the chairs just before my legs went out from under me.

"Where is Henry?" I asked. "I received his letter. He gave me this address."

"Did the letter say it was from him?" Hyde asked as he dipped a small square of cloth into the basin and wrung it out.

"What? No, I recognized his writing. I'd know it anywhere."

Hyde paused for a moment and then turned and handed me

the rag, which I pressed against my face. The cool water soothed the ache some.

"I'm sorry, but you're mistaken," Hyde said. "I wrote the letter."

I stared at him. "No. Henry wrote it. I'm certain."

Hyde looked around the cramped room and shrugged. "He isn't here."

A ripple of disappointment rushed through me, and I leaned back in the chair. "You wrote the letter? And asked me to meet you here?" I wanted to cry. "And where is here, anyway? What is this place?"

"The woman who answered the door is named Helena Carmichael. She takes in young girls who have been otherwise abandoned. People around here seem to think this place is a brothel, but the dagger she keeps on her thigh and the Smith and Wesson in the hall closet beg for people—men—to rethink their assumptions."

"I see," I said. "But what are *you* doing here?"

"Helena took in Mrs. Jekyll when she was a girl for a period of time. It's a bit of a favor. I needed some space. Some time away from Dr. Jekyll." He took the damp cloth from my hand and wiped my face. "What happened to you?"

I shook my head. "It doesn't matter." I couldn't get the image of Sir Carew's wild eyes out of my head. I began to tremble and clutched my hands together to try to make it stop.

"Someone did this to you," Hyde said. His gaze moved to the wound over my eye. He used the damp cloth to wipe the dried blood from my neck. "I think those men who were chasing me when you and I first met would have liked to do something similar to me."

"You should be thankful they didn't have the chance," I said as another shock of pain ripped through my temple.

"And you couldn't run?" Hyde asked. "You couldn't escape?"

I laughed and not because anything about the situation was funny, but because of how absurd he sounded. "Run where? I work for the man."

Hyde stiffened. "Sir Carew did this to you? You would think a man in his position would be aware of the many eyes on him at all times."

"He doesn't care who knows. In fact, I think he's emboldened by it." I sighed. "Sir Carew is well-known. He's rich. He has the kind of influence that regular people can scarcely understand." My throat tightened, and tears clouded my already skewed vision. "Do you know what it's like to be trapped? To know that you won't be seen or heard even if you ever worked up the nerve to say something?" I pressed my hands to my mouth to keep from screaming. "I see the fear of this man in other people's eyes. What chance do I have when others have seen the horrors he commits and are still unable or refuse to do a damn thing about it?"

Hyde was silent, his expression tight as he struggled to contain something within himself—rage, anger, I couldn't be sure.

There was a sudden knock at the door. I jumped up and scrambled back against the wall. It had to be the authorities coming for me. Sir Carew must have called them and sent them to follow me. Could they have found me so quickly? And in this part of town that most people tried to avoid?

"Please, Utterson," Hyde said. "Sit."

"It could be the police!" I scream-whispered. "Sir Carew sent them here!"

"For what?" Hyde asked. "*He* assaulted *you*."

"As if they'd believe me? All he needs to say is that I provoked him or made some threat against him and his actions would be justified."

Hyde stared at the door, his fists balled at his sides. "Let them come."

My heart galloped in my chest as Hyde yanked the door open.

Helena stood in the hallway. "I brought you a present," she said, staring directly at me and shaking a small compact in my direction.

She swept into the room and sat down on Hyde's bed. He closed the door and stood with his back against it.

Helena patted the bed. "I won't bite. Sit down and let me stitch that cut."

I obeyed as she opened the compact in her lap. From it she took a glinting curved needle and a spool of black thread. She laced the thread through the needle and pushed me backward until I was lying flat on my back. She lit a match and held the needle over it for several moments, and then she pulled a tiny clear bottle from some hidden pocket in her dress.

"What's that?" I asked.

"Carbolic acid," she said. "It'll keep your wound from festering."

I didn't know why Helena kept a bottle of surgical disinfectant in her dress, but I was in too much pain to question it. Hyde handed her the dampened rag, and she poured a little of the liquid onto it then pressed the cloth to my wound.

It felt as if she had inserted a red-hot poker directly into my eye. I cried out in agony. Helena held my arm firmly. After a moment the pain began to dissipate, and I took a deep, wavering breath. If I had been standing, I would have fainted.

"Best to distract yourself now, love," Helena said. "It's a nasty wound, but the edges are clean."

"So it won't hurt much to stitch?" I asked.

She laughed. "Oh, it's going to hurt, my darling boy. But it'll be pretty."

She pressed the wound's edges together and my vision went white with pain. I cried out and suddenly Hyde was sitting next to me, his hand on my arm.

I tried my best to put my thoughts elsewhere, but I flinched with each pinch of the needle and the subsequent tug as she knotted the sutures.

"I still don't understand why you've asked me to come," I said to Hyde, trying desperately to distract myself. "How did you know where my rooms were? And how did you manage to fake Henry's writing so perfectly?"

"Henry told me where you stay," Hyde said. "And I didn't fake anything. I wrote the note and asked you to come because I believed you to be in danger. Now I see I was correct, but my efforts were too late."

Another tug of the thread and my stomach turned over.

"Almost done," Helena said. "Six or seven more to go."

That didn't sound like almost done to me.

"What kind of danger?" I asked through gritted teeth.

"From Carew," Hyde said flatly. "As soon as you told me you worked for him, I became concerned. Every young man who finds themselves under his watchful eye is in danger."

"You're right about that," said Helena. "He's got a reputation, but he's rich and still rubbing elbows with the most powerful people in the country." She looped the needle through the skin of my eyebrow and my vision doubled for a brief moment. "Breathe," she said calmly. "Just breathe."

"And so you asked me to come here," I said to Hyde. "Carew tried to force himself on me. I pushed him away more out of instinct than anything else. He was enraged that I dared to bleed on his floor."

Helena took a long, deep breath and let it hiss out from between her teeth. "I wish you'd managed to push him in front of a speeding carriage. We might have gotten lucky and had a Clydesdale flatten his skull."

"Helena—" Hyde interjected.

"Don't chastise me," she snapped, snipping off the last bit of thread. "That man is a predator of the highest order. A wolf."

"A monster," I said quietly.

Hyde stared into the hearth as the orange flames lit up the room. "Are we not all monstrous in some way?" he asked.

"Some of us are, but it is because we have been made monstrous by the world." Helena stood up and pressed out the front of her dress. "Sir Danvers Carew is a monster by choice. He enjoys inflicting pain and humiliation on others. There may be salvation for the rest of us, but not for him." She gave me a quick nod and left without another word.

I reached up and touched the expertly sutured skin running along my brow. I glanced at Hyde, who still seemed distant. In profile something struck me—it was again, familiar. The slope of his nose, the way it connected to the skin above his top lip. The firelight reflected off something propped in the corner of the room just behind Hyde. Dr. Jekyll's cane.

Dr. Jekyll.

I suddenly realized that it was in Henry's father that I'd seen that familiar collection of features. I'd been a fool not to see it before. This would have explained everything.

"You're Dr. Jekyll's son, aren't you?" I asked.

Hyde turned to look at me, and for a moment I second-guessed myself. I'd come to the wrong conclusion, but as the silence stretched on, I thought my theory had to be right. It would explain why he knew so much about the Jekylls, why he was so close to Henry. The ins and outs of it weren't clear to me, but the silence was confirmation enough.

"Curious," Hyde finally said. "Very curious."

"You don't deny it?" I asked.

Hyde stood and went to the door. "You should go. It's already very late. Helena can arrange a carriage to take you back."

"I've offended you," I said. "That was not my intent."

"I'm not offended," Hyde said, but he didn't move from the door. He was still asking me to leave.

A part of me didn't want to return to Miss Laurie's. Maybe Sir Carew had sent the authorities there. They could have been rifling through my things at that very moment. I shut my eyes as I thought through the consequences of the night's events.

"You looked pained, Utterson," said Hyde.

"Sir Carew will end my clerking position," I said as I stepped into the hallway. "He already said as much. He'll make it impossible for me to stay in London. Everything is going to change and I—" I shook my head. "I don't know what I will do."

Hyde put his hand on my shoulder. "I'm sure it will all work out for the best."

"How can you say that to me?" I asked. But as I turned around for an answer, Hyde shut the door in my face.

———

Helena had one of her neighboring tenants take me home. The carriage bumped over the roadway, leaving my head aching and a sick feeling in my stomach. When he dropped me off, Miss Laurie was waiting with her arms crossed and a scowl that made the lower half of her face look like it might slide off her skull. She looked me over and took stock of my injuries, then rushed me inside and had me in a fresh set of clothes and under a stack of warm blankets in record time.

She asked me what happened, and all I could tell her was that I'd be leaving her boardinghouse soon and that I was sorry for breaking her rules about curfew.

"I've never held you to it," she said. "I don't care what has happened, Gabriel. You will always have a place here and I will not have it any other way unless you tell me you're returning to your mother and father."

I started to protest, but she told me to be quiet as she fussed over my bloodstained clothing.

She and I were both in tears when she left my room but we'd come to an agreement. I'd take her up on her offer to stay as long as she allowed me to pay her a fair rate. She begrudgingly accepted, but I had a feeling she would find some excuse to slip any money I'd give her back into my pocket.

Everything would change. The time when it was just me and Henry against the world was over, and I had no idea how far Sir Carew was willing to go to make sure my life would be forever ruined.

As I drifted into a fitful sleep, I could feel something growing in the pit of my stomach—a cold dread unlike anything I'd felt before.

Something awful was coming.

CHAPTER 15

The Terrible Business of Sir Carew

The incessant knocking was accompanied by a familiar voice. He wasn't yelling, but it sounded as if his mouth were pressed directly to my door.

"Open the door, cousin," Enfield said. "Get up and open the door."

I didn't want to. The pounding in my head worsened every time I rolled over or blinked or breathed. Nothing made it better except for silence—which Enfield had thoroughly disrupted—and darkness. The dawning London sky was quickly erasing that comfort and I finally resigned myself to sitting up.

I dragged myself to the door, unlocking it and returning to my bed as Enfield slipped in and immediately locked it again. I glanced at him and he caught sight of my wound. His face twisted up.

"Who did that to you?" he asked, clenching his fists at his sides.

"I don't want to talk about it right this moment. I just want to go back to bed."

"Fine," Enfield said, grasping the handle of my door. I thought he would leave me to sleep, but instead he pulled the handle roughly, making sure it was locked.

I peered at him from beneath my heap of blankets. "Is something chasing you, cousin?"

It was then that I saw he had something rolled up in his hand. A newspaper.

Enfield sat on the edge of my bed and shoved the paper toward me. "Can you even see out of that eye?"

"Barely," I said.

"You need to read the paper. Right now."

I unrolled the rumpled copy of the day's *Daily Telegraph*. I sat up and smoothed it out on my lap. As I read the headline, my blood ran cold and a sick, sinking feeling invaded every part of my body. My heart pounded in my head and made my temples throb, the wound over my eye aching fiercely.

I read the words aloud just to convince myself that it was real: "Sir Danvers Carew Found Slain, Murderer on the Loose."

"Read on, cousin," Enfield said.

A maid, Miss Carolyn Prichard, in the employ of one Sir Arthur H. Thurman, was sat by her window late the previous evening. She was mending a blanket and heard a commotion coming from the street below. The Thurman residence is near the docks and several pubs and so it was not unusual to hear all manner of ruckus from time to time. Miss Prichard ignored the first shouts and only went to her window when she heard a man calling for help.

It should be noted that an especially gray fog was rolling through the city at the hour and her view was partially obstructed, but she claims to have seen an older man in a traveling suit and a tall black hat as he quarreled with another man in a black frock coat and a black or possibly dark brown bowler.

Miss Prichard could not clearly make out the subject of their argument but claims to have seen the older man put his gloved finger in the other man's chest at which time the assailant produced a cane and hit the older man repeatedly about the head and neck until he collapsed. Miss Prichard claims the assailant beat the older man until he stopped moving and then fled the scene on foot.

Miss Prichard promptly alerted the authorities. Upon their arrival the deceased victim was identified as Sir Danvers Carew, a prominent practitioner of law, and board member of the London School for Medical Studies, among other prestigious positions.

The assailant has yet to be identified. Authorities are asking for the public's help in apprehending this vicious criminal. They hope that this account and the information provided therein will be of some import, and anyone who has additional information should contact the police at once.

Orbs of light danced through my vision, and I realized I was holding my breath. I gasped as I took in the macabre illustrations accompanying the report. A broken and battered Carew lying facedown on the paving stones, a faceless assailant standing in the background holding a cane high over his head.

The last image was a photograph of the cane the assailant had allegedly used to murder Sir Carew; he'd apparently left it behind when he fled. The bloodied instrument was slender, made of wood, and broken in half by the force of the beating.

But the handle, an intricately carved bird's head with eyes made of gemstones, was instantly recognizable.

It belonged to Dr. Jekyll.

"Can you believe it?" Enfield asked. "The old man is dead." He gave me a gentle pat on the back, and I turned to meet his gaze. There was understanding there, though I'd never spoken explicitly about what I'd endured at the hands of Sir Carew. "Give yourself some time to think it all through. I'm sure you'll be able to find another clerking position soon. And when your father finds out, I'm sure—"

I cut him off before he could say anything else. "No."

A look of concern spread across Enfield's face. "No, what? What is it?"

"You don't understand," I said through gritted teeth, my hands trembling. "I was at Sir Carew's office. I was working and he'd been drinking and he tried to put his hands on me. When I denied him that, he struck me with a candlestick."

Enfield's mouth opened and then his jaw clamped tight. His eyes flitted to my wound. "I hope he's gone straight to hell. I wish the murderer all the good fortune in the world." He suddenly sat bolt upright. "Cousin . . . did you—"

"I didn't kill him," I said quickly.

It was clear I'd picked the thought straight from his head because he sighed in relief. "Right. I may not have blamed you, but still."

There was another knock at my door. Enfield got up to answer it, and Henry ducked into the room.

I stared at him as if he were a ghost—from the looks of him he may have already had one foot in the grave. He was gaunt, the hollows of his cheeks deep, the wells under his eyes dark.

"My god," Enfield said. "Jekyll. What in the world has happened to you?"

"I need to speak to Gabriel," Henry said. "Alone."

Hearing my name from his lips sent a ripple of warmth through me. Everything that had happened between us was not forgotten but I was ready to forgive all. Enfield looked to me and I nodded. He left, closing the door behind him.

"I've been trying to speak to you," I said, unsure of where to start. "It's been months, Henry. I've written to you. I went to your house."

"I know," Henry said. He approached me slowly. His clothes hung from his bones like he was made of sticks and flesh and nothing more. His dark hair looked like it hadn't been cut in a month. He stood in front of me with his hands in his pockets. "Sir Carew."

I held up the newspaper. "Henry, your father's cane is pictured here. It's the murder weapon."

Henry raised his hands, palms out. "Please lower your voice."

I was already whispering, but I lowered my tone even further. "Do you know who did this?"

Henry sat down next to me, and having him so close brought on a deluge of emotion. I wanted to put my arms around him and tell him how much I'd missed him. I also wanted to shake him and demand that he explain himself.

"What are your thoughts on the matter?" Henry asked. He did not look at me as he spoke, his voice shaky.

I set aside my grievances with Henry for the moment and thought the situation through. Dr. Jekyll was a strange man, but not a murderer.

"I believe it was Hyde," I said.

Henry's head snapped up.

I should have thought it through more, but I'd always been in the habit of speaking plainly to Henry. "What are the odds that another person has a cane like the one used to commit the murder? How many men are walking around with *that* sort of stick?"

Henry looked down at the floor. "You don't know that. It could have been anyone."

"Henry," I said. "I saw Hyde in possession of the cane last night. I saw it in his rooms in Christ Church."

"You were in his rooms?" Henry asked.

"I . . . Yes. I thought you'd be there." I suddenly felt an urgent need to explain myself. "There was a letter here. I thought you wrote it. It was in your hand." My head throbbed. "I was mistaken. Hyde was there and I saw the cane."

Henry's normally luminescent brown skin was ashen, drained. "Do you enjoy his company?"

I was blindsided by the accusation. All I'd ever wanted was Henry. I'd been driving myself mad trying to understand his relationship with Hyde, making myself sick as I pictured them together, and ultimately deciding that I cared enough about his happiness to allow him that without any interference from me. And now Henry was accusing *me* of favoring him? "You can't seriously believe that."

"It's not really about what I believe," he said flatly. "It is about the truth." He moved toward the door. "You've been in his rooms. You met him in the alleyway near my home. You think I don't know?"

"I went to both those places for *you*! I wanted to see *you*!"

Henry shook his head. "I didn't understand how this would unfold. That you would actually prefer him. Curious."

"How what would unfold?" I asked, a sudden panic gripping me. "I don't prefer anyone to you. Henry, please, be honest with me. Tell me who Hyde is to you. Is he your father's son? Does your mother know?"

"Stop," Henry said. "I made a mistake. I'm sorry, Gabriel. Truly. I wish things could be different, but they cannot." He straightened out his coat that was now two sizes too big for his frame. "Rest assured I will have my father deal with Hyde."

He rushed out, and as I stood to chase him, a wave of nausea knocked me back.

"Henry!" I called as the room began to spin. I shut my eyes and lay back. Footsteps sounded in the hall and my heart leapt, but it was only Enfield. I sank back into my blankets.

"I've never seen Henry run so fast. What did you say to him?"

An idea suddenly struck me, and I pulled myself up to sitting even as every muscle in my body protested. "I need to write a letter. Can you have someone deliver it? I need it done today. As soon as possible, but it must be done with the utmost secrecy. Can you arrange it?"

"Yes," Enfield said, a look of absolute confusion stretched across his face. "Is everything all right?"

"No," I said. "No, it is not."

I borrowed a pen and paper from Miss Laurie and drafted a letter.

> *Hyde,*
>
> *I care only for Henry. I want to make that very clear. He has some other idea stuck in his head and I hope it is not because you've led him to believe otherwise. I have also come to believe that you may have something to do with the death of Sir Carew. What is the truth? What are you hiding and how is Henry involved? Send word to me when we should meet so that you may give me the answers I seek.*

I left the letter unsigned, put it in an envelope, and gave it to Enfield along with the address in Christ Church.

———

Henry's wide eyes stayed in my mind as I tried to sleep away the pounding in my head. Miss Laurie brought me soup on a tray and insisted that I drink a steaming cup of warm milk. The bitter aftertaste warned me she'd added something to the drink, and I soon found myself drifting in and out of consciousness.

When I was finally able to open my eyes, I found myself in the company of two men in uniforms and one very angry Miss Laurie.

"This is my place," Miss Laurie said. "I don't appreciate you harassing my guests."

"We'll ask our questions and be on our way," one of the men said.

I sat up. Only a faint ringing remained in my head. The pain over my eye was less. I was disoriented, but soon found that I was still in my room, tucked beneath my covers.

"Get up," the shorter man said. He pulled my blankets aside and tossed them onto the floor, then pulled me roughly up by the arm.

"I'll not have you treat him this way!" Miss Laurie chided.

The taller officer shoved Miss Laurie out of the room and slammed the door.

"You belonged to Sir Carew?" The shorter officer had a badge with the last name *Carlisle* stenciled across it. "Answer me."

"No," I said firmly, "I'm a clerk in his practice." I resented the implication that I was somehow his property and that's exactly why he'd phrased it that way. He was trying to provoke a reaction.

The taller officer, the name *Landry* on his badge, picked up the newspaper Enfield had left behind. "You've seen the news then?" he asked.

I nodded. "A tragedy." I hoped my expression didn't betray me.

"Indeed," said Officer Carlisle. "A fine upstanding man such as him deserved better than to be beaten to death in the street. Speaking of which, where were you last evening?"

"Here," I said quickly. One thing I'd observed from my time

in Sir Carew's office was that he immediately assumed the worst when one of his clients took too long to answer a simple question. "After I left Sir Carew's office for the evening, I had my wound stitched and then I came here." There was no sense avoiding it and I thought if I brought it up first it might curb their suspicions.

"And where exactly did you get that wound?" Officer Carlisle asked, as if I'd somehow asked for the gash in my face.

"I fainted at Sir Carew's office. I hadn't eaten. I blacked out, made a mess of the ink. There was blood everywhere."

The officers looked at each other.

I touched my head. "Sir Carew was not happy about my wasting his ink and ruining his notes, so I assured him I would make it right by replacing the wasted supplies. I need to be careful about getting up too fast when I haven't had enough to eat."

The officers were completely disarmed.

"So you don't know what happened to him?" Officer Landry asked.

"He insisted that I tend to my wound and sent me away without another word." I held my head in my hands. "I won't be able to make it up to him now." I pretended to be on the verge of tears. "I hope you catch the person who did this."

"Do you know if Sir Carew had any enemies?" Officer Carlisle asked.

It took everything in me not to look at him like he'd grown another head. Of course the man had enemies. He wielded the law and his unchecked power like a weapon. Even people who put him on a pedestal hated him.

"He was a lawyer," I said. "I would have to think he made some enemies along the way."

Officer Carlisle's face fell like he'd just thought of how many suspects that would leave him to follow up with.

Officer Landry folded his hands together in front of him and glanced at the other policeman. "We've got other leads to follow up with in Christ Church." He turned back to me. "We'll be on our way, but let us know if you think of anything else that might be helpful."

I nodded, but my heart stuttered at the mention of Christ Church. They already suspected someone there of being involved, and the odds were long that it could have been anyone other than Hyde.

CHAPTER 16

ℭHE ℒABORATORY

MISS LAURIE'S POTION, WHICH SHE CONFIDED IN ME WAS LACED with rum and a few drops of laudanum, had kept me in a sleepy haze. So much so that as Officers Carlisle and Landry left the boardinghouse, I realized it was well after noon.

My head still swam—whether it was from my injury or Miss Laurie's drink, I couldn't tell. I washed my face, dressed, pushed a hat down on top of my head to try to hide my still-weeping injury, and left as Miss Laurie pushed a buttered roll into my hand. I took a few bites and tossed the rest aside, a sick feeling stuck in my gut as I made my way to Leicester Square.

I needed to talk to Henry. Now that the police seemed to suspect Hyde, the situation was much more precarious than it had been before. There would be real consequences for killing a man like Carew. Never mind the fact that Carew was a monster—if the killer was a young Black boy, they could very well skip any sort of due process and lynch him the way Charles Woodson had been only a year prior. Woodson had been an innocent bystander during a conflict between sailors outside a pub in Liverpool when the mob turned on him and chased him until he ended up in the water at Queen's Dock. The crowd then stoned him to death as he tried desperately to swim away. No part of me wanted to see Hyde subjected to a similar fate, regardless of what he may have done.

Stranger still, if Hyde was responsible for Carew's death, I didn't understand his motive. What I'd shared with him had been jarring, but had it made him want to track Sir Carew down and murder him? He had no obligation to me. Our interactions had been strange and intense, and I left each of them feeling like I'd had a conversation with a ghost, but there was *something* there between us. I could not name it. It was a familiarity, though he was mostly a stranger to me. It was a certain comfort that I found in him, but there was also terrible unease.

When I arrived at Leicester Square in the late afternoon, I went straight up the front steps and knocked. Mr. Poole answered a moment later.

"Mr. Utterson," he said.

"Don't tell me he isn't here," I said. "This is very important and it cannot wait."

"Dr. Jekyll has instructed that I allow no one in while he is away. He's taken Mrs. Jekyll to her mother's home for an extended visit."

"Mrs. Jekyll is gone? So Dr. Jekyll isn't home?" I asked, peering around him.

"That's correct," Mr. Poole said. He pushed the door open wide. "Should you happen to come in while my back is turned, then I technically haven't allowed you in at all."

I quickly went in and he closed the door behind me. I glanced at the narrow cannister holding the various canes and umbrellas. The bird-handled cane was, of course, missing.

"Young Henry is in the laboratory," Mr. Poole said.

He gestured for me to follow him, and he led me through the house to the rear door. We hurried across the garden to the laboratory entrance. I'd never been to that area of the Jekyll estate, and as I followed along behind Mr. Poole, I suddenly felt that awful sense of unease, as if I were treading into an area that I ought not. I even detected a sense of hesitation in Mr. Poole; his pace slowed and his gait shortened as if he didn't want to proceed.

The entrance to the laboratory was a windowless metal door, which Mr. Poole unlocked with a key he'd pulled from his pocket. Upon entering the cramped entryway there was almost no light. All the windows were shuttered. A thin sliver of daylight filtered through a crack in one of the wooden slats. There was nothing in the entryway save a small table with a candle and a box of matches. Mr. Poole lit the wick and dancing shadows sprouted all around us.

"The laboratory is off-limits," Mr. Poole said. "I only have a key to the outer door we've just come through. But this is where Dr. Jekyll, young master Henry, and Hyde spend nearly every hour of the day."

I followed Mr. Poole down a short, narrow hall, at the end of which was another windowless door. There was a sudden hitch in Mr. Poole's breathing, and he stopped just outside the door. He knocked. There was no answer.

He knocked again. "Master Henry. You have a guest."

"I told you I was not to be disturbed," Henry growled.

I stepped to the door. "Henry. It's me, Gabriel."

There was a pause, then shuffling.

"You'll excuse us, Mr. Poole," Henry said, his voice much closer to the door now.

Mr. Poole handed me the candle, then turned and left.

"Open the door," I said. "I must speak with you about Hyde."

"We've already spoken about him," Henry said. "What more is there to say?"

"Please, Henry, open the door."

There was a long pause and then a series of clicks. His footsteps moved away, and I pushed the door open.

Dr. Jekyll's laboratory was unlike anything I'd ever seen. From my schooling I'd, of course, seen other labs, and there were things I recognized: test tubes, beakers, various liquids in a vast range of colors, shelves full of books.

What struck me about Dr. Jekyll's lab was the disarray. Organization in a lab was paramount. It was one of the first lessons we'd learned in chemistry: Stay organized, otherwise deadly mistakes would be made. But there was no sense of organization there. In fact, it was the complete opposite. There were so many vials and beakers crowded together on the various tables, so many open notebooks, funnels, and scales, glass flasks and cork stoppers. There were implements everywhere, crowding every surface. Papers sat in piles on the floor. A large blackboard covered in scientific equations far more advanced than anything I could interpret sat against the wall.

Henry had taken a seat on a stool in the farthest corner near a smoldering fireplace. At his feet were rumpled blankets, like someone had been sleeping there recently. A large mirror also stood against the wall.

"Henry, what is going on here?" I asked.

"This is my father's lab," he said in a flat, emotionless tone. "He pours all of his brilliance into this place."

"His brilliance?"

"My father is a brilliant man," he said.

"I know. I didn't mean anything by it." Henry had always been in awe of his father. He put him on a pedestal.

"I'm sure you didn't." Again, his voice was flat, barely changing tone or inflection. Even the look on his face was unmoving.

Something was very wrong. He was changed somehow. And it wasn't just his thinning frame or his sunken eyes. It was something else—something I could not identify.

"I need to speak with you about Hyde," I said.

Henry shifted on the stool. "I assure you he has been dealt with. He is gone and I do not think he will return."

"Gone?" I asked, confused. "He was able to make passage so quickly? Where did he go?"

"It makes no difference," Henry said.

"He is guilty then?" It seemed that if he left town, then he must have been involved and was looking to escape the inevitable consequences.

"I cannot make a judgment against him," Henry said as he reached into his coat and produced a letter. "This came in the morning's post."

I slowly approached Henry and took the letter. I opened it and read the short note in the neat scrawl. I almost handed it back to Henry, thinking he'd given me the wrong paper—it was his handwriting.

I glanced at it again.

No. Not his handwriting. But similar enough.

My dear Henry,

I have gone and do not intend to return. I have caused you enough strife. I am sorry. All I ever wanted was to help in any way I could. You need to be whole, Henry. Someday, I hope you will be.

Hyde

I couldn't understand. "He's really gone then?"

"This bothers you?" Henry asked. "I asked you before if you had developed some affection for him. I see now that my suspicions were founded. It's fine." He smiled, but the way his mouth twisted up was like a puppet—stiff and unnatural and most definitely not fine. "I want very much for you to be happy. Can you be happy now, Gabriel?"

"I don't know what you mean," I said. "Why are you acting like this? I told you I had no affection for Hyde other than a sort of curiosity. I care for you and you alone."

"We are friends," Henry said.

I felt like I'd been struck in the face.

"Of course we're friends, but I . . . I thought—"

"Enough of this, my dear Gabriel," Henry said, taking me by the shoulders. "Let the past stay in the past. We will move forward as fast friends, you and I, but nothing more."

All the world felt as if it were crashing down on my head, my heart breaking apart in my chest.

I had hoped that we could begin again. But that hope bled out of me in a river of unstoppable tears.

"This is what you want?" I asked through a choked sob. I stared into Henry's unblinking eyes. There were no tears there, no sadness, and none of the despair that crept under my skin and burrowed itself deep.

He leaned forward. "It is all I have ever wanted."

The rush in my ears made my head ache. I staggered back as if he'd hit me. He hadn't, and yet he had wounded me in a way that hurt even more than what Sir Carew had done to my skull.

I turned and left the laboratory as fast as my unsteady legs would take me. Henry didn't follow, but he did close the door upon my exit and lock it.

I stood alone in the darkened hallway. Without the candle, the darkness swallowed me whole.

I stumbled out into the garden where Mr. Poole waited. He locked the outer door and took me by the elbow, leading me inside the main house where he sat me on a chair.

"Calm yourself, Mr. Utterson," he said. He put his hand on my shoulder. "What has happened?"

"Hyde is gone," I said.

One of the women in the kitchen stuck her head out and Mr. Poole shooed her away.

"Master Henry told you this?" Mr. Poole asked.

I realized I still had the letter in my hand. I gave it to Mr. Poole and he read it.

The color drained away from his face. "Where did this come from?"

"Henry said it came in the post this morning."

"No," Mr. Poole said, handing the letter back to me. "I took in the post this morning, and this was not among the correspondence. And does it not look similar to Master Henry's own hand? Come now, Mr. Utterson! Something foul is afoot here!"

"Shhhhh!" the woman from the kitchen hissed.

Mr. Poole quieted himself. "I'm sorry, but this letter came from inside this house, and I suspect that Master Henry and Mr. Hyde have been conspiring to craft this ruse."

"What ruse?" I asked. "He's Dr. Jekyll's son, is he not?"

Mr. Poole's face fell. "That is a scandalous accusation and I'd appreciate it if you never spoke of such things again—in my presence or anywhere else for that matter."

Mr. Poole had been with the Jekylls for twenty years. If anyone knew the truth it would have been him, but the suggestion seemed ludicrous to him. In his mind, it was an impossibility.

"I'm sorry," I said. "It's just that he and Dr. Jekyll look very much alike. You don't see that?"

Mr. Poole said nothing.

I stood and tucked the letter into my pocket. "I need to go."

Mr. Poole nodded. Then he took my place in the chair, holding his head in his hands.

I let myself out, and as the cool, crisp air filled my lungs, I could not help but feel overwhelmed by my circumstances. Hyde was gone, Carew was dead, and Henry was changed in a way that both hurt and confused me. I should have let it all go, but I could not.

I touched the letter in my pocket. There was something I needed to know, and this letter from Hyde, in his own hand, would help me find the answer.

CHAPTER 17

ᴛHE MATTER OF THE LETTERS

THE LONDON SCHOOL FOR MEDICAL STUDIES WAS A PLACE OF many disciplines. In preparation for entering the medical field, students there learned to catalogue and count surgical instruments in hopes of one day becoming surgeons themselves. Students learned the form and function of the organs and musculoskeletal structures. If there was interest in apothecary work, the study of chemical compounds would commence. Dr. Jekyll had taught those classes, and Henry and I had sat in rapt attention.

When I was dismissed from school, I learned that there was a similar place for people who wanted to learn the ins and outs of the law before going on to study it formally. There were also departments dedicated to the study of other more specific disciplines, including the science of handwriting analysis. I knew of only one person who was an expert in that field.

Mr. Guest was an expert in handwriting analysis, as evidenced by his work with Sir Carew on the matter of Mr. Hopkins. It was for that reason that I sought him out to help prove my own suspicions—that Henry had forged the letter from Hyde in an attempt to cover for him. Why he would do such a thing was beyond me, but my gut was telling me that it was where I needed to start.

I found Mr. Guest in his offices in Belgrave Square. The little bell above the door clanged as I entered. Mr. Guest was hunched over a wide desk, a pair of magnifiers perched on the bridge of his nose. Several handwritten documents lay scattered in front of him.

"How can I help you?" he asked without looking up.

"I'm not sure if you remember me. I'm Gabriel Utterson."

He glanced up. "You're Sir Carew's clerk. Or . . . you *were*."

I nodded. "Yes, sir."

"Seeing as the man is dead I doubt he has any more work for me." He shrugged. "He paid me half of what he agreed to the last time he was in need of my services."

"I'm here on my own behalf," I said.

"Is it a legal matter?"

I chose my words carefully. "No, but I suspect that a friend of mine may be in some kind of trouble. I need to know if he wrote this." I took out the letter.

"I charge a fee," Mr. Guest said. "But seeing as how the old miser is dead, I'm feeling quite generous. Let's have a look."

I joined him near his desk and handed him Hyde's letter.

"I'll need something to compare it to," he said.

I always kept Henry's letter in my breast pocket, the one where he spoke of what we would do in the future, of how much he cared for me. I hesitated.

Guest narrowed his eyes at me. "I'll assume the sample document is of a *sensitive* nature?"

I nodded, avoiding his eyes.

"I am a professional," Mr. Guest said. "And I have seen things committed to paper that would make you wish you didn't know how to read."

"It's nothing like that," I said, though I felt he was trying to put me at ease. "It's a love letter. To me."

"Ah, love," Mr. Guest said, clasping his hands together dramatically. "I can guarantee you it is nothing I haven't seen before."

He stuck out his hand and I set Henry's letter in his upturned palm.

He pushed aside his other documents and laid the letters next to one another. He traced over the opening words of Henry's letter first.

"And you want to know what exactly?" he asked.

"I need to know if they were written by the same person."

Mr. Guest nodded and leaned in close as he examined the ways in which the letters were constructed, muttering to himself the entire time.

"Upstroke on the long arm of the letter *R*. Quite unusual. Loop across the top of the *o*, crossbars connected with stems."

He leaned so close his nose was nearly touching the paper. "Do you see this?" He picked up an uninked pen and used the dry tip to indicate where I should focus.

"What am I looking for?" I asked, peering down at the letter.

"The small bloom of ink on the last letter of this word and then the unusually disproportionate period. The person slowed down here and paused before he continued. This letter was written with care."

Heat rose in my face, but Mr. Guest didn't notice as he turned his attention to the Hyde letter.

"This writing is very similar." He traced over the letters. "These two are most definitely authored by the same hand, though he tried very hard to disguise it."

My heart sank. Henry *had* forged this letter. And now there was no way to know if Hyde was truly gone.

I shoved my hands in my pockets and shook my head. My fingers brushed against something I'd forgotten was there—the note Hyde had written to me asking me to meet him in Christ Church. I took it out and stared at it for a moment before setting it next to the other letters.

"What about this one?" I asked. I'd been so sure the handwriting was Henry's that when Hyde confessed to writing it, I had thought he was lying.

Mr. Guest looked back and forth between the letters and after many minutes of silence, punctuated by grunting and mumbling to himself, he sat back and huffed.

"What is it?"

He took off his magnifiers and replaced them with a pair of round spectacles. "All three of these documents were authored by the same person."

I touched the note Hyde had admitted to writing. "I know for certain that this one was written by someone else."

He shook his head. "No. It was written by the left hand of the person who wrote the other two."

"What?"

"Is the person ambidextrous?" Mr. Guest asked. "It's very rare to be able to write so fluidly with both hands."

"No—No, this note is written by another person."

Mr. Guest turned to me. "Am I the expert here, or are you?"

"You are. Of course. But I—I know who wrote it. He told me himself that he penned it."

"Then I'm sorry to say you are being lied to, Mr. Utterson. Do these two have some kind of vendetta against you? Do they enjoy making you look foolish?"

I took all three documents from him and put them in my jacket pocket.

Hyde could imitate Henry's handwriting, and Henry could imitate Hyde's. It made no sense at all.

"Can two people learn to mimic each other's writing? Is it

possible two people could be equally good at forging each other's script?"

Mr. Guest huffed. "It's nearly impossible for one person to fake another's handwriting. I would say that is an impossibility."

"Thank you for your time," I said. "I think I've made a mistake."

Mr. Guest sat back in his chair. "You're sure it's two people?"

I nodded. "There is no doubt."

"People who are related sometimes have very similar writing," he said. "They would have had to have been educated near one another from a very young age, but even then, that does not account for the level of similarity here."

"I think they may be brothers," I said.

Mr. Guest looked thoughtful, then after a moment shook his head. "No. That wouldn't explain it."

There wasn't much else to say. "I'm sorry to have wasted your time."

"It's fine," he said. "Seeing as how Sir Carew is probably lying stiff on a mortician's table, you're out of a job."

I glanced up at him. "He paid me a pittance and my family paid *him* for the opportunity."

Mr. Guest looked dumbfounded. "Slavery was abolished in Britain by 1833 and slavery-like apprenticeships were finished in 1840."

"I think Sir Carew knew that as well as anyone," I said.

"Knew, didn't care, and still found a way to do it." He rolled his eyes and tossed his spectacles down on the table. "Do you want a real job? With wages? Where you don't have some beastly man glowering at you all day?"

I could scarcely believe what he was saying.

"I worked for Sir Carew for a month after I finished my studies." Mr. Guest turned and looked me directly in the eye. "Maybe you'll raise your glass to toast the glorious occasion of his gruesome death, then you'll think on my offer and let me know what you decide."

He stuck his hand out and I shook it. Mr. Guest returned to his work and I left his office in a daze. I wanted to run to Henry and tell him the news—the thought brought with it a dizzying crash.

Henry was pulling away from me, and the revelation that he may have written all the letters, possibly even with Hyde's knowledge, was almost too much to bear. It made no sense that he would do such a thing. Hyde had admitted he wrote the note that led me to his room in Christ Church, but perhaps it had been Henry all along.

CHAPTER 18

The Hunt for Hyde

WANTED FOR QUESTIONING IN THE DEATH OF SIR DANVERS CAREW

HYDE

An investigation and subsequent autopsy have determined that Sir Danvers Carew was killed with malicious intent. Authorities are now seeking the man generally known as Hyde. The suspect is of indeterminate age, but appears to be less than twenty years and stands 5 feet 10 inches. His defining feature is a shock of white-gray hair. He is believed to be extremely dangerous.

Four weeks have passed since the murder and the investigation is now at a standstill. London Criminal Investigation Department

**detectives are asking anyone with informa-
tion to avoid a direct confrontation with the
suspect. The public is being asked to stay
alert and report any sightings of the suspect
to the proper authorities.**

The general consensus was that Hyde was a bloodthirsty monster and that he had killed Sir Carew in a fit of uncontrollable rage. That may have been true, but the local papers made it seem as if Hyde might be lurking in the shadows and would kill again if he wasn't apprehended soon. The murder weapon had been traced back to Dr. Jekyll, who claimed it had been stolen by Hyde, who was working in his laboratory as an assistant.

Henry ceased all contact with me. No letters, no visits. Nothing. And I didn't call on him. He kept his distance and I did the same, because what more was there to say?

———

I buried myself in work, having taken Mr. Guest up on his offer. My father was only slightly more disappointed than he usually was at the news. He no longer needed to pay Sir Carew or Sir Hastings, and the position with Mr. Guest was paying me enough to cover the cost of extending my stay at Miss Laurie's through the spring, though she went to great lengths to avoid taking money from me.

I couldn't ignore the situation entirely. The gossip surrounding Hyde's alleged crimes was everywhere. People in areas all across the city claimed to have seen Hyde, and the accounts grew stranger and stranger as time went on. A woman in a small dockside community said she'd seen him stalking the streets, looking to snatch young children. A man in the East End said he'd seen Hyde leaping from rooftop to rooftop in the light of a full moon like some preternatural creature. Each false claim cast him in a more monstrous light than the one before it.

While I had many questions about Hyde and his connection to Henry and Dr. Jekyll, I didn't believe most of what was being said. If he had killed Sir Carew, and I sincerely believed that he did, I feared he'd only done it because of me. I'd unknowingly gone to him after Sir Carew attacked me. Hyde had seemed disturbed by the brutality of it, and yet I still could not understand why he felt an obligation to me strong enough to defend me— strong enough to take the life of the man who had hurt me.

I tried my best to bury those questions and the thousand others I had. My work was time-consuming and required focus. I was all too happy to devote myself to it completely. The only other thing that helped was a newfound connection with my dear friend Lanyon. He'd been quite ill lately and I'd spent nearly every evening with him at his home—walking in the garden or playing with his younger sisters in his stead as he sat on the bench and watched on.

When he was feeling better, he invited Enfield and me over

for what he assured us would be just a small dinner for a few of his close friends. When we arrived, Enfield was delighted to find the home filled to bursting with guests. My cousin loved a good party, and while I preferred to be in my room with a good book, I was looking forward to checking in on Lanyon.

Enfield spotted a game of charades being played in the garden and went to join in while I sipped cider and listened to a man play lively tunes on a fiddle. As I watched the musician tune his instrument and tap his foot to lead into his next song, a hand grasped my shoulder. I turned to find Lanyon grinning at me.

"I'm so glad you've come," he said. His words ran together a bit—clearly he'd already indulged in the festivities, maybe a little too much. "I've been bored without you."

"Bored? With a house full of guests?"

"These people are here so they can say they attended a party at the famed Lanyon estate." He took a wobbly step back.

"What makes you think I'm not here for the exact same reason?" I asked, taking hold of his arms and steadying him.

He feigned being hurt, placing his hand on his chest. "I knew it! You don't really like me at all. It was just a trick to get yourself invited to one of my very famous parties."

He was joking but it still stung. I would never do anything quite as shallow as that. Even in his hazy state, he must have seen something change in my expression, because he suddenly swept me up in a tight embrace.

"My dearest Utterson. Forgive me. The drink is quick and

it is winning the race with my better mind." He pulled back, but our faces were still very near to each other. I could smell the sweet scent of white wine on his tongue. I could see the heat blooming in his cheeks, a ruddy deepening of his warm brown skin.

"Perhaps you should sit," I offered.

"Perhaps I should stand right here and look at you," Lanyon said. "You have ever been a friend to me, Utterson. I feel foolish not having seen it before."

"Seen what before?" I asked.

"Just you," he said.

I let my gaze wander to the floor.

"I've embarrassed you," Lanyon said. "I'm sorry."

"I'm not embarrassed. I'm flattered."

When I looked up again Lanyon was staring off, his gaze leveled at the entrance behind me, and I realized the giddy chatter had ebbed. I followed his line of sight, and there in the doorway was the last person I expected to see.

Henry.

Lanyon sighed and stepped away from me. After a rush of whispers rippled through the crowd, people turned their attention from Henry back to their drinks and dancing. I could not.

Henry met my gaze across the room and cut a path straight to me. His gaunt face had filled out some, but his eyes still looked sunken and sad.

"Mr. Utterson," he said.

I nearly flinched at the sound of my name from his lips. He almost never called me Utterson, and never with a formal title attached to it.

"It's very good to see you, old friend," he continued.

"Is it?" I asked before I could stop myself. "I haven't heard from you in weeks, but it's very good to see me?"

Henry's face contorted into a mask of confusion.

Lanyon let his shoulder press into mine. Henry's gaze flitted to him and then back to me, his expression unreadable. I could not get past the look of him—his normally brown skin was ashen, tiny red veins traced through the whites of his eyes, and his lips were dry and chapped.

"It's very good to see you," he said again in the exact same tone he had just used. Like he was reading the words from a script and not like he really meant them.

"Are you well?" Lanyon asked, an edge of annoyance in his voice. "Do you need to sit down?"

Henry shook his head. "I'm better than I've ever been. Everyone thinks so."

"What?" I asked, confused. "Henry, *no one* has even seen you."

"If they had, I doubt they'd agree that you are better than you've ever been." Lanyon wasn't even trying to hide his disdain. "Do you need a balm for your lip? Maybe some water?"

Henry's head whipped around, and he smiled in a way that made me take a half step back. His eyes were dull and glassy.

"Would you like to sit with me?" I asked hesitantly.

Lanyon gave a small huff and took up a seat on a chaise. Henry moved to a winged-back chair by the fireplace as the crowd ebbed and flowed around us, enjoying their drinks and merriment.

I didn't know what to say to Henry. I'd tried to put him out of my mind, but I would have been a fool to think I could keep it up forever. Even as I sat in the chair closest to him, I felt the familiar stir in the pit of my stomach. Despite the strange new state of our friendship—if that was all he wanted it to be—the memory of his embrace lived and breathed in every fiber of my being. Memories washed over me like a flood, reminding me of the way Henry's affection had been the only thing that kept me afloat for so long.

But as Henry avoided my gaze and sat with his body angled away from me, the warm memories subsided, replaced with a drowning sorrow that rushed in like the high tide.

"How have you been?" Henry asked Lanyon.

Lanyon raised an eyebrow. "I've seen better days." He rested his back on the arm of the chaise and crossed his legs. "The doctor says I'm to be on bedrest for the foreseeable future."

"Then why are you having a party?" Henry asked.

"I'm saying farewell to the fun," Lanyon said. "Sending it off with a bang." He pulled at the collar of his shirt like it was too tight.

"Why are *you* here?" I asked Henry. "I don't think I've ever seen you at one of these get-togethers."

"No?" Henry asked, like he wasn't sure. He shrugged. "I'm turning over a new leaf. New beginnings. Things like that."

He seemed so fragile, as if he were made of paper. I gripped my hands together to keep from reaching out to touch him.

"How is your father?" Lanyon asked.

"He's well," Henry said. "He's been working. He's so busy, he has barely the time for anything else. I have to remind him to eat most nights."

"What is he working on?" Lanyon asked. "And he's doing this work from your home? Is he being paid?"

Lanyon was very forward, and Henry seemed to take exception.

"What he does in his lab is none of your business," Henry snapped.

Lanyon looked him over from head to toe, sizing him up. Then he laughed. "Jekyll, I could not care less about what fringe science your father is undertaking in his dusty old lab."

Henry stood straight up, pushing the chair backward.

"*Fringe?*" he asked angrily. "My father is doing the work that everyone else in his field is afraid to do. His work will remake the world."

"In what way?" Lanyon asked, leaning forward but not standing up.

"Your father is very proud of you," Henry said suddenly. "You are very lucky. Not everyone has that privilege."

Lanyon looked as confused as I felt. Henry's father was a highly intelligent, highly accomplished man. He was also incredibly hard on Henry, but I never got the impression he didn't care for him. Quite the opposite; Dr. Jekyll was obsessed with the success of his son. He pushed for him to have every possible opportunity.

"Your father loves you, Henry," I said.

Henry glanced down at me. "He does. And that is exactly why he has undertaken this work. It has consumed him."

"What work?" I asked, standing to face him. This time, I reached out and touched his hand. He pulled away immediately.

"It was a mistake to come here. I should be going." He turned and headed for the door.

I started after him. "Henry, wait—"

He dashed out into the street and I followed him. Carriages lined the road, their horses moored to posts. Most of Lanyon's guests were inside, but a few still milled about in the chilly night-time air. I cautiously approached Henry as he stood staring up into the sky, breath coming in billowy clouds.

"I wish you could understand," Henry said quietly. "I wish I could make you see."

"I might be able to if you would just talk to me," I said. "Tell me what is happening. What is this work your father is doing, and what do you mean it will remake the world?"

Henry laughed lightly. "I misspoke. I meant to say that what he is attempting may remake *his* world."

"I still don't understand." I walked around Henry so I could look him in the face, but he kept his eyes to the sky. In his right hand he held a small, flat-bottomed glass flask filled with a dark purple liquid. He quickly stopped up the opening with a cork and shoved the flask into his pocket.

"Henry?"

He sighed, and I noticed that his lips were tinted violet.

"You should not look at Lanyon the way you do," Henry said. "And you shouldn't look at me that way, either."

My throat was suddenly tight, and anger bubbled up inside me. "I don't need you telling me who I can and can't look at, or how. When I look at Lanyon, he looks back. He doesn't make me feel as if I've done something unforgivable simply by caring for him."

Henry's expression remained blank.

"What happened to you?" I demanded. "I need to know why you've become so distant. This isn't you. This isn't who you used to be."

"I *have* changed, Mr. Utterson. You may wish to change, too, someday."

My anger flared. "No. I don't want to change. And you're not just distant, Henry. You're cold. Dismissive. You act like I'm not standing right here in front of you pouring my heart out!" I had to stop and gather myself as a few of Lanyon's guests watched us from the long shadows cast by the streetlights. "You are changed, Henry. Don't you see that? I want to know why."

"I am changed," he said. "But for the better."

"Better? You think treating me this way is *better*?"

191

Henry sighed and looked upon me with such pity I was struck silent.

"I'm not treating you any kind of way, Mr. Utterson. I am simply treating you the way I should have this entire time—as a friend, and nothing more."

That cut deep, but it was not the real issue. "I want to be your friend. Of course I want that, but where have you been? Why have you locked yourself away? What has changed so much between your letters over the summer and now? And where is Hyde?"

Something sparked in Henry's eyes at the mention of the other boy.

"It makes sense that you'd wonder where he is. But I cannot tell you because I do not know. What I know is that he's gone, and he's taken all of his reckless behavior with him. I hope he is gone forever."

There was no reason to believe the authorities would ever catch up with Hyde. There had been no news of him, and his image and sensational story had already begun to fade from people's memories. Hyde's alleged actions had freed me from Sir Carew's grip. The crime was despicable, but a part of me was thankful.

"I need to go," Henry said. "Take care, Mr. Utterson."

I watched him walk down the street and disappear into the thick nighttime fog. Maybe Hyde was gone forever, but it seemed the Henry I had known—*my* Henry—was gone as well.

CHAPTER 19

LANYON'S SECRET

THREE WEEKS LATER, I SAT AT MY DESK IN MR. GUEST'S OFFICES and held a letter in my hand. Not the kind I needed to put under a magnifier and analyze. No. This letter was sure to be of a personal nature. The return address was in Cavendish Square, delivered by courier that morning.

I opened it and read the shaky script.

> *Gabriel,*
>
> *You must come to me at once. It is of the utmost importance. Tell no one where you are going. Burn this letter after you've read it.*
>
> *It is in regards to our friend H. I fear I have no time left. Please hurry.*
>
> *Lanyon*

As soon as I'd cleared my desk of the day's work I set off for Lanyon's home with a stone in the pit of my stomach. The weeks since Lanyon's party had not been kind to me—I thought of Henry and the way he'd acted that night, but more than that,

I thought of the way Henry had been when we first met. He'd changed so drastically that I scarcely recognized him anymore. We were not friends who had simply drifted apart or outgrown the need for each other. With Henry, it was as if he'd woken up one day and decided all the things that had come before, all the time we'd spent together and the things we shared, didn't matter.

I arrived on Lanyon's doorstep and knocked. A tall, slender woman with a severe chin and narrow eyes opened the door. I'd never seen her before, but she looked old enough to be Lanyon's mother.

"I'm Gabriel Utterson. I'm here to see Lanyon, ma'am."

"He's expecting you," she said. She turned and gestured for me to follow her.

The house was eerily quiet, except for a strange noise coming from somewhere on the second floor. It was an awful noise—like a gasp of steam escaping from a kettle, except instead of a whistle there was only a dry rasp. And it kept repeating. Over and over again.

As the woman led me up the steps, the front door opened and Lanyon's younger sisters came in. They were dressed in black, and their normally giddy chatter was replaced with a soft whimpering. Crying.

"This way," the tall woman said. "You'll need to be quick."

The strange sound repeated. On the second floor landing it was more pronounced. I could not think of what could be making it, but as we moved toward a door at the end of the darkened hall, it grew louder.

The tall woman stopped just outside the last door on the left. The sound was coming from inside. She put her hand on the knob, took a deep breath, and pushed the door open.

I struggled to make sense of what I was seeing. A person lay on their back in the four-poster bed. A gasp rattled out of their throat and into the open air. It was a horrible, wheezing sound as the air was sucked in and blown out with great difficulty.

"I'll give you some privacy," the tall woman said. She put her hand on the center of my back and gently nudged me toward the figure in the bed.

I stood confused for a moment until I noticed the person's head—topped with a mass of dark brown curls.

"Lanyon?" I asked aloud. No. This could not be my friend. The figure in the bed was a husk. A hollowed-out shell of what had once been a vibrant young man.

I approached the bedside, and he turned his face to me. I clapped my hand over my mouth to keep from screaming. Was he dead and somehow reanimated? No—that couldn't be, but it made no sense to me that this corpse had enough life left in it to move under its own power.

"Gabriel," Lanyon's voice broke from the figure's lips like smoke, thin and wispy. "You've come."

"Lanyon." I could think of nothing else to say. I had not seen him since the night of the party. I'd been so busy with work and when I was not working I slept. I hated myself for not coming to see him sooner.

"There is no time," he said between heavily labored breaths. "I'm dying. I am already dead."

I went to his side and reached for his hand, but stopped when I saw how emaciated he'd become. His bones showed through his skin, which was stretched far too thin.

Tears stung my eyes. "What has happened to you?" Was it a question I was fated to ask of every person I'd ever cared about?

"No time," Lanyon croaked. "Listen to me now." He sucked in a hollow breath and blew out. His breath was rancid, a sure sign that his insides were already beginning to rot.

I held my breath to keep the vomit from climbing up the back of my throat but made no move to step away from him.

"After the party, you left. Jekyll left. I wanted to—" He paused and took several breaths, one after the other. "I went to Jekyll's one week ago. I—I wanted to confront him about how awful he'd been to you."

I set aside my fear and clasped his hand in mine. It was cold and stiff, his fingers curled into a ball. Lanyon clung to his mortal body, but it would not be long. He was dying right before my eyes.

"Mr. Poole showed me in," Lanyon continued. "I waited at the door—the laboratory door. Jekyll allowed me in. I yelled at him. Cursed him for being so terrible to you. He did not deny it."

A stab of pain in my gut. I had questions, but I would not interrupt what I felt certain would be Lanyon's last words.

"Something . . . changed." Lanyon coughed and sputtered.

He rolled onto his side toward me, reached out with one bony appendage, and grasped my shirtfront with more strength than should have been possible given his terrible condition. "My heart, Gabriel. I was already sick. But I saw . . . something. I saw Jekyll, he—he changed."

"I know," I said through my tears. "He is different—"

"No!" Lanyon cried, shrinking back against his pillow. "Not only in his ways, but in his body. I saw him *change*."

"I don't understand."

Lanyon closed his eyes and his breaths came in long draws with even longer pauses in between. "Hyde."

I leaned in closer, ignoring the stench of decay. "What about Hyde?"

Lanyon opened his eyes and tilted his head toward me. "I wrote you . . . follow the instructions, Gabriel. To the letter."

"Lanyon, I don't—"

"Promise me," Lanyon said, gripping my hand. "Swear it."

I put my other hand over his and clasped it tightly as I could without feeling as if I would snap his frail wrist. "I swear."

I did not know to what I was swearing, but if it was what Lanyon needed to hear in that moment, I would say it.

He seemed to relax some. He closed his eyes and let himself sink into the bedclothes. Lanyon's lips parted. He inhaled deeply and the last bit of breath bled out of him. It felt as if someone had stood and walked out of the room.

Lanyon was gone.

CHAPTER 20

A HORSE-DRAWN CARRIAGE LED THE PROCESSION OF MOURNERS through the streets and into Highgate Cemetery. I had borrowed a suit that was a size too big from Enfield for the occasion. My cousin joined me in my grief—Lanyon had been a friend to us both.

I walked behind Lanyon's mother, who was eerily silent. His father wept openly, as did his sisters who, upon seeing me, had rushed forward and buried their tearstained faces in the folds of my jacket. I didn't know what to say to them, and so I let my tears mingle with theirs.

Tucked among the moldering tombstones and shadowy mausoleums was the Lanyon family crypt. There, people spoke kindly of Lanyon and lamented his tragic loss—a loss that I was still struggling to understand.

When they pushed the black box containing Lanyon's mortal remains into the wall of the crypt and sealed the space with a heavy concrete block bearing his name, his mother fainted and had to be carried away.

The mourners trickled out as a light rain spattered the stone pathway, turning it from dull gray to shiny black. I stayed when everyone else had gone. Enfield offered to stay, too, but I insisted that he leave. I needed a moment alone.

I laid my hands on the tomb and pressed my face against the broad marble facade. I stared up into the gray sky as the smell of damp earth mingled with the faint stench of decay.

I shut my eyes. My chest ached and my heart was weary. None of this made any sense, and the grief was almost too much to bear. Curiouser still was the dreadful manner of Lanyon's passing.

Lanyon's father had told me that his son had been recently diagnosed with a condition of the heart, and had been ordered by his physician to stay in bed and not exert himself in any way. One evening in the weeks before his death, Lanyon had told his mother he had grown bored and went for a walk. He returned hours later in such a state of ill health that they fully expected him to die that same evening.

But he held fast and asked for pen, paper, and a courier.

His last act was to send for me.

————

In my room at Miss Laurie's, I sat in a daze when there was a small knock at the door. Miss Laurie stood on the other side with a letter in hand.

"This arrived for you just now," she said. She put the envelope in my hand and reached up to set her palm on the side of my face for a moment, then shuffled away.

I sat down and read the return address on the letter.

It was from Cavendish Square.

Lanyon.

My hands began to tremble so violently I had to set the letter down for a moment to gather myself. I'd racked my brain in the previous days trying to understand Lanyon's last words to me. He said he'd written to me and asked me to follow the instructions. This must have been what he meant.

I slipped my finger under the seal and took out the contents. The first item was a single sheet of folded paper. The second was another letter sealed with a wax stamp.

Lanyon's scrawl ran across the folded page, something he must have written in the last days of his life.

Gabriel,

I must ask you to trust me. If you can do that, please proceed. But if you cannot, throw the contents of this letter and the other into the fire unopened. It is not too late to turn back. I fear that if you do not, you will be irrevocably altered by what I will share with you.

If you have read this far, then I will assume you have considered the risk and are willing to proceed. My instructions are these: Open and read the enclosed letter ONLY upon the disappearance or death of our dear Henry Jekyll.

This is all I can say. I am not long for this world, my dear Gabriel.

I remain most truly yours,

Lanyon

I snatched the other letter up and began to break the seal, but stopped as Lanyon's face pushed its way to the front of my mind. His pleading eyes in those last moments would live forever in my memory. In that moment I had sworn to him that I would do as he asked. I had given him my word, but his note seemed to imply that Henry was in some kind of danger. Death or disappearance? No matter how far we had grown apart, I couldn't imagine having to bury him as I had Lanyon.

I pushed the thought out of my head, secreted Lanyon's sealed letter under my mattress, and went to call on Enfield.

CHAPTER 21

INCIDENT AT THE WINDOW

"YOUR GRIEF HAS GOTTEN THE BETTER OF YOU," ENFIELD GRUM-bled as he tripped along behind me. "What are we going to do when we get there? Yell at him? Tell him he's a terrible person for not coming to Lanyon's funeral?"

"We need to end this right now," I said. "I believe Henry may be in danger. I need to know what all this secrecy is for. Why does he disappear for weeks on end, then show up and act like a completely different person? And Hyde—"

Enfield huffed. "Please tell me you're not still going on about him. Let it go, cousin. He's on the run. If they ever catch him, they'll execute him for what he did to Carew."

I stopped and rounded on Enfield. "Then I hope they never catch him. I hope he finds some place to live out his days in peace and happiness. The world is a better place without Carew in it."

Enfield's eyes grew wide. "I know you're angry——"

"Anger isn't even the half of it." I turned around and kept walking. "Are you coming with me or not?"

He quickened his step, walking along beside me. We stayed silent until we emerged in front of Henry's house.

"The carriage is gone," I said. There was no movement from the windows, no smoke from the chimney.

I crossed into the alley that abutted the Jekyll residence and found the door to the rear entrance to the laboratory locked.

Enfield heaved a sigh. "We can't just let ourselves in."

I searched for another entrance and found the garden gate sitting slightly ajar. I slipped into the inner courtyard and Enfield came in behind me.

"We'll be arrested for trespassing," Enfield hissed. "This is dangerous."

He was right, but I didn't care. I needed to know why Lanyon thought Henry might be in danger.

Someone cleared their throat and drew my attention up to an open window on the second floor of the house. There in the window behind a gauzy curtain sat Henry.

I gazed up at him and he locked eyes with me. My blood turned to ice in my veins. Henry sat with his arm propped on the sill, his dark eyes wide and blank. He still looked as ill as he had the night of Lanyon's party, but now the hollows under his eyes were so deep the sockets looked almost empty.

The hair on the back of my neck stood on end as his lips

pulled back over his teeth in what was meant to be a polite smile, but turned instead into some nightmarish grin.

"You've come to visit me, Mr. Utterson?" Henry asked. Even his voice sounded strange. There was a ring of something familiar in it, something of his old self, but it was masked by a terrible rasp.

"Mr. Utterson?" Enfield's brow furrowed and he tilted his head to the side. "Why are you calling him that?"

"It is the polite thing to do," Henry said from the window. "Titles are important."

Enfield looked like he wanted to snatch Henry right out of the window, and I was suddenly glad he was out of reach on the second floor.

"How very kind of you to stop by," Henry said. "I trust you'll be on your best behavior, otherwise I'll have to call for your removal."

"I don't know what you mean," I said.

"Oh yes you do," Henry snapped. "Don't come around looking at me with those big eyes. They betray you and all of your terrible yearnings. I want nothing to do with it."

I had never felt such anger and it burned through me like a raging fire.

"We buried Lanyon," I said. I didn't swallow my sorrow or the stifling sense of betrayal. I wanted Henry to see it. I wanted him to feel it, if he still could. "I miss him so much I can hardly breathe! It hurts, Henry!"

"He was a friend to you," Henry said flatly. "We are all in need of friends every now and again."

"Stop speaking to me like that!" I screamed. I couldn't hold it back a moment longer. "Stop speaking to me like you don't care if I live or die. Lanyon is *dead*! He was my friend and he was yours as well! You didn't even come to his funeral!"

"I wish him a peaceful rest," Henry said. "You should do the same, and then you should move on."

"Move on?" I asked, stunned by his frigid demeanor. "Move on from what? From caring about people? I do care, Henry! You used to care! What is *wrong* with you?!"

Enfield put his hand on my arm. "This is pointless, cousin. He isn't the Jekyll we know. Not anymore."

I wrenched my arm out of his grip and positioned myself under the window, as close to Henry as I could manage without disappearing from his line of sight.

"Lanyon was worried about you. I'm worried about you." I let the tears stream down my face. "I need you to remember who you are, Henry! You are not this!"

"How would you know what I am?" Henry asked as the curtain billowed in front of him. He didn't move. He didn't even tilt his head to look at me. "You can't know what I've become."

There was a commotion in the room behind Henry, and Dr. Jekyll's face suddenly appeared in the window.

"Gabriel?" he asked. He looked surprised to see me. His expression immediately soured. "Get off my property this instant."

I looked to Henry, who didn't even blink.

"What has happened to him?" I shouted. Enfield pulled me toward the garden gate, but I planted my feet. "Why is he like this? What did you do to him?"

"What did *I* do?" Dr. Jekyll put his hands on the sill and leaned out. "This is *your* fault! This would not have been necessary if you hadn't corrupted him!"

"All I have ever done is care for Henry!" I shouted.

"You think I'm a fool?" Dr. Jekyll asked. "I've seen your letters. Your incessant pining drew Henry into something he should never have been a part of in the first place!"

The world around me went silent. My breath caught in my throat.

Henry said he'd burned our letters.

"Get away from me and my son and never come back," Dr. Jekyll said. "You should be ashamed. Look at the harm you've done. Look what has become of my dear boy, all thanks to your reckless influence."

He slammed the window shut. Enfield tugged me back another step—in that moment I was utterly incapable of doing anything on my own. All I felt was white-hot rage.

Henry had only ever strived to please his father. The pressure he put on himself to live up to Dr. Jekyll's unattainable standards was crushing. And then there was his father's attitude toward *us*. What I realized in that moment was that of course there had been an *us*. It wasn't my overactive imagination: It was real, and what had existed between Henry and me meant something even if his father didn't want to acknowledge it.

Dr. Jekyll was behind this. And I had no doubt that Henry was following along with it, because all he ever wanted was to make his father proud of him.

In that moment all I wanted to do was leave, but something caught my eye. As I peered up at the now closed window, I expected to see Dr. Jekyll's ruddy face, his eyes full of anger and malice. Enfield also looked up, and what we saw in that moment was something I could not fully explain.

Henry stood in the window looking down at us. He narrowed his eyes at me and something shifted in his expression— no—not his expression.

His face.

His jaw seemed to widen, pushing out at the high points of his cheeks and just under his bottom lip. His eyes became rounder and more widely set. A guttural noise erupted from his chest and he gripped the windowsill. His normally close cut and tapered hair seemed to lengthen, and as the daylight slanted through the window, the color seemed to change as well. The bones of his face were changed. The muscles stretched in tight ribbons down his neck, the skin pulling so tight I thought it would split open.

I blinked repeatedly. It was the grief. It was a state of shock at witnessing Lanyon's death firsthand. It was the agony of seeing him put in a box and sealed up in a tomb at Highgate Cemetery.

But Enfield gasped beside me. He gripped my arm so tight I thought it would break.

Henry raised his hand, grabbed the edge of the curtain, and drew it closed.

I raced out of the garden and into the alleyway, Enfield hot on my heels. We ran out into the main street and did not stop until we got to St. James's Park.

I collapsed onto a bench and put my head between my knees, my heart beating against my ribs. Sweat dripped from my forehead and dampened my shirt.

Enfield sprawled out on the ground and covered his face with his hands. "Gabriel—"

"Don't," I said. "Don't say anything right now. I don't know what just happened and I'm afraid that if we speak of it, I will go out of my mind. Just wait. Please."

Enfield rolled up to a sitting position and pulled his knees to his chest, rocking from side to side like a child. The minutes ticked by and still we said nothing. I felt the gentle breeze on my skin, let the chirping of the birds fill my ears. I forced myself to listen to their songs, allowed myself to wonder what kind of birds they were and if they were staying to make nests in the trees.

"Gabriel." I hadn't noticed Enfield had come to sit next to me on the bench. "We need to discuss this right now."

I didn't want to talk about it. I wanted to stay lost in my own thoughts where I could choose to think of the birds and the trees and not of the impossible, horrifying thing I just witnessed. But Enfield would not let me.

"Tell me what you saw in the window," I said. "Do not embellish. Do not soften it. Tell me exactly what you saw."

"It was Henry," Enfield said, his bottom lip trembling. "At least I think it was. I saw him standing there, but the curtain was in the way. The sunlight—the shadows. It was a trick of the light."

"No. Don't do that. Don't try to rationalize it. It wasn't the curtain. It wasn't the light."

"Then what was it? What are you suggesting?"

I didn't know. I had no idea what I had just seen in Henry's face. I had no explanation for it. My mind immediately went to my own fragile state. Everything had been like an exposed nerve since Lanyon died—raw and painful. Nothing made sense anymore, and here was yet another thing that I had to try to figure out. I didn't want to do that, so I turned my attention away from that horrid image of Henry's face contorting and focused instead on Dr. Jekyll's venomous words.

"You heard what Dr. Jekyll said about me. Do you think he was right? Do you think it's my fault that Henry is so distant and strange?"

"What?" Enfield asked. I know he was expecting me to tell him what I thought I'd seen in the window. When he realized I was not going to address it in that moment, he sighed as if he too wanted to put it out of his head. "I don't think you would ever do anything to hurt him. I know how you feel about him. I thought I knew how he felt about you. I don't think I'm wrong, but clearly his father must've seen something in it that caused him to act that way."

Tears welled up and I swallowed hard. "What did he see? That I loved Henry? That I cared for him? Is that wrong?"

Enfield let his shoulders roll forward as he took a deep, mournful breath. "I think it depends on who you ask. You know very well what people say. People are willing to close their eyes to things they do not agree with, but it requires you to make yourself invisible. Maybe your affection for Henry was a little too obvious for Dr. Jekyll's liking."

I clenched my jaw against a fresh stab of anger. "Do you know what was obvious? Sir Danvers Carew putting his goddamn hands all over me, and all over any other person in his sight. He did that right out in the open and everyone knew about it. That didn't offend their delicate sensibilities, but my affection for Henry did?"

"I didn't say I agreed," Enfield said. "I'm only telling you what Dr. Jekyll might have been thinking."

"What is Dr. Jekyll doing to him in that house?" I asked.

It was the only question that mattered in that moment. Lanyon had feared for Henry's safety and now, so did I.

CHAPTER 22

Mr. Poole Has Something to Say

Eight days passed after the incident at the window. Enfield
and I did not speak of it, and I didn't breathe a word to anyone
else. I didn't dare. I didn't return to the Jekyll residence for fear
of further angering Henry's father, but I thought of little else.

I had convinced myself that what I had seen at the window
was only in my mind, my grief over Lanyon's death playing a
cruel trick on me. That Enfield had seen it, too, was a complica-
tion that I was happy to overlook. Enfield himself was convinced
that while we had both seen the change in Henry's face, it was
simply a trick of the light as it shone through the gauzy curtain.
He refused to discuss it further, and that was fine with me.

What I could not set aside was the look on Dr. Jekyll's face
and the accusations he had hurled at me.

I sat curled over a will that one of Mr. Guest's clients was convinced had been forged. The man had died and left everything

to his new wife and their infant son, excluding his children from his previous marriage altogether. I was going to have to inform them that it wasn't a forgery—their father was simply a petty, childish man. Of course it was always possible that the man's older children had been excluded for a reason, but it was not my job to determine if that was true or not.

The bell over the door clanged as someone came into the office. Mr. Guest was scheduled to consult with three clients that day, but was not expecting the first until well after noon. I glanced up and recognized the squat little man standing there: Mr. Poole. And he looked as if he'd seen a ghost. His skin was ashen, his dark eyes peeled open as if he were afraid to blink. He shuffled over to my desk.

"Mr. Poole?"

He set one trembling hand on my shoulder. "Mr. Utterson. I'm sorry to call on you unannounced, but I was hoping I could have a word."

I tried not to show how shaken I was by his request. It couldn't have been anything good, not with that look of utter terror stretched across his face. I excused myself and led Mr. Poole outside and across the street to a wide expanse of green space. Mr. Poole sat on a bench but I stayed standing.

"Is it Henry?" I asked, holding my breath.

"Yes. But I am at a loss for what to do. I know you and Master Henry were once very close. You might be still if Dr. Jekyll—" He clamped his mouth shut. "I cannot speak ill of my employer.

I simply have nowhere else to turn and I cannot involve the police. This matter is entirely too . . . sensitive. Or perhaps too strange. I don't know, but I am certain there is much at stake."

"Mr. Poole," I said. "What has happened?"

Mr. Poole looked around and, seeing that no one was anywhere nearby, gestured for me to join him on the bench. I sat and he leaned close to me, making his voice a whisper. "Henry has locked himself in the laboratory. I have not seen him in eight days."

"What do you mean you haven't seen him? Surely he comes out to eat. To sleep."

Mr. Poole shook his head. "You would think that, wouldn't you? But those would be the actions of a normal person, of someone who had nothing to hide." He shook his head and sighed. "Can you come with me now? Right this moment?"

I hesitated. "Where are we going?"

"To the laboratory," he said. "I cannot say more unless you come with me."

"Wait here," I said.

I quickly spoke to Mr. Guest, collected my jacket and hat, and met Mr. Poole outside. We took a carriage to the Jekyll residence. When we arrived, Mr. Poole led me through the front door and down the center hall to the kitchen where the entirety of the staff was huddled together. Whatever conversation they were having immediately ceased as I entered. They shared a collective expression of fear—all pinched mouths and furrowed brows. The tension in the air was palpable.

"I must admit that this is highly unusual," Mr. Poole said, wringing his hands. "I'll take you to the laboratory now."

I could not shake the creeping dread that slowly burrowed its way under my skin.

Mr. Poole leaned close to me. "And when we arrive at the inner door, I would ask that you say nothing. Just listen. Can you do that?"

"I don't understand. Didn't you say Henry was locked in there? And where is Dr. Jekyll?"

"Dr. Jekyll left eight days ago. The same day I watched Henry go into the laboratory, and as god as my witness he has not emerged since that time."

Eight days ago.

The very same day I'd seen Henry at the window. The worsening crush of fear was suffocating.

Mr. Poole started for the rear door. "Please. Come with me."

We walked out the back door and through the garden. The towering Golden Rain trees displayed coral-pink leaves and yellow flowers, but remnants of their shed foliage from autumns past lay scattered across the ground, and they crunched under my boots as we drew closer to the laboratory's outer door. Mr. Poole retrieved the key from his pocket, his hands trembling so violently it took him three tries to get it in the lock.

As we passed through the outer door, the entryway was much as it had been the last time I set foot inside, only this time the dark was more complete. The windows had been shuttered then, but now they were also boarded up from the inside so that no trace of daylight might enter. It smelled of heat, dust, and some pungent chemical aroma that reminded me of embalming fluid. A shudder ran through me, and I had to lock my knees to keep them from knocking together.

Mr. Poole struck a match and lit the candle on the small table. He held it high as we proceeded down the narrow hallway. Save for the silhouette of Mr. Poole in the dim candlelight and the thin ribbon of muted light coming from under the door at the end of the hall, I could see nothing.

We stopped in front of the inner door, and Mr. Poole pressed his finger to his lips in a plea for me to keep quiet. I nodded. He raised his hand and knocked three times on the door.

"Master Henry," Mr. Poole said loudly. "I've come to inquire about what you'd like us to prepare for dinner. Mrs. Lennox is willing to make you anything your heart desires." Mr. Poole's tone was light, almost playful, but his face was a mask of tightly controlled fear.

Footsteps sounded from behind the laboratory door. A shadow moved in the faint glow emanating from underneath it.

"I'm not hungry," came a growling, angry voice.

The skin on my arms rose to gooseflesh, and the hair on the back of my neck stood up.

"Come now, Master Henry," Mr. Poole urged. "You must eat something. Would you like a glass of water or perhaps some soup?"

"I cannot be bothered! Leave me!" There was a hard thump against the door and the footsteps retreated.

I was about to protest and opened my mouth to speak when Mr. Poole grabbed me roughly by the arm and motioned for me to remain quiet.

"Very well," Mr. Poole said.

He ushered me back down the hall and led me across the garden and into the main house. As we settled in the kitchen where the other staff were still gathered, they watched me with expectant, terrified eyes.

"Tell me, Mr. Utterson," said Mr. Poole. "Whose voice was it that you heard in the laboratory?"

I gripped the edge of the counter to keep myself upright. I knew the voice, and it was not Henry's. It was Hyde's. But I could not bring myself to say so aloud.

Mr. Poole watched me as the realization sank in: Not only had Hyde returned, but he was now lurking in Dr. Jekyll's lab and answering Mr. Poole as if he were Henry.

Mr. Poole perched himself on a tall stool, and Miss Sarah, another member of Dr. Jekyll's staff, brought him a steaming mug of tea, which he gulped down. "Eight days ago, in the very late evening, Master Henry and Dr. Jekyll quarreled. They spoke of promises made and unmade, of Henry's weaknesses, of Dr. Jekyll's disdain of Henry's affection for you."

I stiffened, a rushing sound filling my ears.

"They moved into the laboratory, but we could still hear

them screaming at each other," Mr. Poole continued. "And then we heard a sound that was unlike anything we had ever heard before."

"It was awful," said Miss Sarah. "I was a nurse for many years. I've seen terrible things and I've heard all manner of cries, but this was something else. It chilled me to my bones."

"Henry cried out from inside the lab," said Mr. Poole. "It carried up the chimney and we heard it in the garden. It was pain, Mr. Utterson. Like an animal caught in a trap. And then an hour later, Dr. Jekyll emerged and said he had to go on a short trip. He left immediately and assured me that Henry would be spending most of his time in the lab and that we should not disturb him."

Before I could think, I was moving toward the back door. Mr. Poole stepped in front of me. I went to push him out of the way and he grabbed my wrists.

"Listen to me," he said. "You cannot go to the lab and cause any sort of commotion without risking our safety and our livelihoods." He glanced back at the staff, who remained silent. "Dr. Jekyll *will* find out and we *will* lose our positions."

"You've been with the Jekylls for more years than I've been alive," I said. "They would fire you so easily?"

Mr. Poole looked hurt. "Not they—*he*. Mrs. Jekyll has always been kind and fair. It is Dr. Jekyll I am concerned with. Ever since Hyde showed up here, Dr. Jekyll has not been himself, and neither has Henry."

"And you're sure Hyde is not his son?" I asked.

Mr. Poole glanced back at the gathering of household staff; they all looked stunned. He shook his head. "I've already told you my thoughts on the matter. I do wish you would put it out of your mind.

"When Hyde fled," he continued, "we thought we were rid of him. We prayed that things would return to the way they had been before, but things have been worse. Henry is different." Mr. Poole ran his hands over the top of his head. "I can't explain it. He has always been a soft-spoken boy but never dismissive, never aloof. It is as if something has been extinguished within him. I cannot understand it."

I knew all too well what he meant. I'd seen the way Henry had become disinterested in everything—including me. I saw the pain in Mr. Poole's face and I knew I could not go against his wishes, but I also could not leave Henry in the company of Hyde without knowing if he was safe.

"Why has Hyde returned?" I asked.

"I do not know that he ever left," Mr. Poole said. "I have a sneaking suspicion that he has been here the entire time, secreted in the lab."

No . . . that was not possible.

Then again, Mr. Guest—a man I had come to know as reliable and trustworthy—assured me that Hyde's letter and Henry's letter were written by the same person, a left hand and a right hand. Perhaps Henry was trying to cover for Hyde by forging the letter but as I thought on it, what I had seen at the window pushed its way to the front of my mind and made the blood in my veins run cold as ice water.

Mr. Poole sat down again and Miss Sarah went to him and began gently rubbing his back. "Perhaps you should go lie down for a little while."

Mr. Poole nodded and was ushered off by the other staff, leaving only me and Miss Sarah in the kitchen.

"I've known Henry since he was just a small boy," she said, tears in her eyes. "I don't want to go snooping in the laboratory because I am afraid of what I might find." She looked at me with all the concern of a worried parent. "I fear something has happened, and I fear Dr. Jekyll is to blame."

Anger smoldered in my gut and I again moved toward the door, but Miss Sarah stopped me.

"Come back after dark," she whispered. "I will leave the garden gate unlocked. If you are caught, I will deny ever having this conversation."

I gazed out the large window overlooking the garden and the entrance to the lab beyond it. I would save Henry from this place, one way or another.

CHAPTER 23

A Secret Revealed

I DID NOT RETURN TO MISS LAURIE'S AFTER LEAVING THE JEKYLL residence. Instead I stood in the alleyway between the buildings across the street and waited until the dark fell down around me and the fog rolled in.

The lamps went off in the house and the lamplighter put on the streetlights, the gas inside their globes casting a hazy light. Coupled with the fog and the dark, there was a feeling of foreboding in the air.

Carriages still rattled up and down the street despite the late hour. I crept across the road and entered the alley next to the Jekyll residence. I noticed several people milling about, but they were unconcerned with me as I proceeded to the garden gate. It was unlocked just as Miss Sarah said it would be, and I slipped inside. Only then did I realize I didn't have the key to the outer laboratory door. I approached it anyway and found it, too, was unlocked.

I went in and closed the door as quietly as I could. I did not light the candle, and I took care to avoid the boards that had creaked under Mr. Poole's feet when he'd brought me to the door earlier in the day.

The laboratory's inner door was shut; in the shadows the dark wood looked like a gaping void, as if the end of the hall terminated into the mouth of some monster with its jaws yawning open.

At the door I leaned as close as I could, gently resting my hand on the wall to steady myself. There was a rustling behind the door.

And then came Hyde's voice.

"Please, Henry," he said. "Do not do this."

There was a noise—something akin to a growl. I held my breath.

"I have no choice."

Henry was indeed inside, and so was Hyde.

"You do," Hyde said. "But you must be the one to make it."

There was a long pause, the clinking of glasses knocking together.

"I've made the only choice that leaves me with some semblance of a normal life," Henry said.

Another low rumble and then a strangled yelp. I put my hand on the door handle but did not turn it. Not yet.

"Without the person you care for most?" Hyde asked. "What about him? Can't you see what you're doing to him? Is it worth it? To please a man who would rather see you dead than happy?"

Glass shattered behind the door, and I could no longer stay silent.

"Henry!" I yelled. I tried to open the door but it would not budge. "Open the door! I know you're in there!"

There was a commotion on the other side. I took a step back, planted my left foot on the floor, and kicked the door with my right. It cracked along the jamb but didn't open. I stepped back and gave it another hard kick. This time, the frame gave way and the door crashed open.

I rushed in to find the room empty and the rear door to the lab swaying open. I followed, peering into the alleyway, but saw no one.

"Henry!" I called.

"He's gone for the moment, but he will return," Hyde's voice echoed from the lab.

I stepped back inside and turned to find him perched on a stool in the far corner of the room where the shadows were darkest and deepest. There were no lamps lit in there, only the dappled light of the moon streaming in from the single skylight.

Hyde was wearing a rumpled pair of brown trousers and a jacket with a soiled shirt underneath. A large dark stain seeped down from his collar.

"What have you done with Henry?" I demanded.

"What have I done with Henry?" he parroted my words back to me in an amused tone. "I can assure you it is not I who has done anything to Henry. But what has Henry done to me? Have you asked yourself that?"

I wanted to snatch him right off his stool but maintained my composure. "I'm done playing these games. Where is he?"

Hyde didn't move.

"You are a wanted man," I said.

He tilted his head to the side just slightly. "For killing Carew."

"Yes."

"You think me a murderer, Gabriel?" he asked.

My name from his lips struck me silent. It was too familiar, as if he had known me for years, as if it were sacred to him. There was only one person who spoke my name this way . . .

"I—I saw the cane that was used to kill Carew," I stammered. "I saw the very same one in your rooms."

"And that makes me guilty?" he asked.

"I . . . don't know," I said honestly. I'd been so sure, but now doubt had seeded itself in my mind. "I need to talk to Henry."

"He will return. But he is not the same as he was . . . before."

"Before what?" I asked impatiently.

Hyde sighed and tilted his head back, gazing at the skylight. "It is my fault Lanyon is dead."

I stepped back, nearly toppling a large beaker filled with a purple liquid.

"Why would you say that?" I asked. "Lanyon was sick."

"It was his heart," Hyde said. "The strain—it was too much. It was an accident. A terrible mistake."

223

I gripped the edge of the table. "I don't know what you're talking about, but I don't want to hear any more. You're lying to me. You've been lying to me the entire time."

"The only liar is Henry, and he is lying to himself. It is he who has betrayed your trust."

"Don't speak of him that way!" I shouted.

"You are no fool, Utterson," he shot back. "Try to understand that Dr. Jekyll despises everything about his son, and he has used every one of his considerable skills to excise that which offends him. He has very nearly completed the process." Hyde shook his head. "What will become of us if he succeeds?"

I stared into his face, straining against the shadows to get a clear view of him. In the dim light of the cloud-covered moon, I saw a trail of tears cutting a path down his cheek.

I suddenly felt like I couldn't breathe. I should not have come. Overwhelmed and confused, I backed up and raced out the rear door into the alleyway. I wandered the streets of London until the sun warmed the horizon and burned away the blanket of dense fog.

CHAPTER 24

MISS M

I CRAWLED INTO BED AS THE LAMPLIGHTERS WERE EXTINGUISHING the streetlights, but I could not sleep. My mind spun in circles. Each new thing I learned was like a puzzle piece, and I could not see the bigger picture no matter how hard I tried.

The smell of bread coaxed me out of my stupor. As I ate, my fellow housemates chatted about school, about family, about normal, everyday things. I envied them. I hoped there would be a time in the very near future that I could go back to worrying about mundane things, but something in my gut told me that wouldn't happen. As I picked at my food, other boys came and went.

A scrawny younger boy named John lugged in a sack of coal and put it by the hearth. He walked up to me and set a letter smudged with black streaks in front of me.

"A woman asked me to give this to you," he said. He wiped his face with the back of his hand, leaving a streak of black coal dust across his cheek.

"Who?" I asked, picking up the letter.

"Don't know," said John. "She didn't say."

I rushed to the front door and pulled it open, looking up and down the crowded street, but saw no one I recognized. Whoever had delivered the letter was likely long gone.

I took the letter to the front room and opened it.

Seek out Miss M in Harrington's Market. We've been sent there many times to procure something in a closed box. There may be answers there.

Sarah

The time for normalcy had passed. It seemed my life was now a never-ending series of mysteries. All I'd wanted was to have Henry at my side, to study the law, and maybe be able to laugh a little along the way. Henry was gone, my study of the law had been tainted by the horrors inflicted on me by Sir Carew. And laughter? I didn't know if I'd ever find enough happiness past the awful things that had happened. It was all too much and I could feel myself beginning to break.

So I did the only thing I knew how to do: try to figure out what I should do next. I dressed and set off for Harrington's Market with the letter from Miss Sarah tucked in my pocket.

———

When I finally arrived at Harrington's, I immediately bypassed the butcher's and moved through the cramped labyrinth of side streets and alleyways. Miss Sarah had not given an address, but there was no need. It could only have been the place where I'd seen Mr. Poole and Hyde arguing.

At one point I got turned around and wound up someplace unfamiliar, and so I had to backtrack and start over. Finally, I came upon the strange crooked house.

Black smoke billowed out of a chimney that looked as if it might topple over and crush a passerby at any moment. The windows on the upper floors were tightly shuttered.

I climbed the front steps and knocked, having no idea what I would say or if the person inside would admit me. A small slot in the door slid open and a set of wide brown eyes peered out at me.

"What do you want?" a woman asked in a gruff voice.

"I'm looking for Miss M," I said.

She huffed. "Why?"

"I have a very dear friend who is in some kind of trouble, and I—well, I don't know why but some of the staff in his household think you might be able to help me."

"Someone lied to you," she said.

"Do you know Henry Jekyll or his associate Hyde?"

The woman narrowed her eyes at me, then slammed the slot shut.

I sighed and stepped off the front stoop. Another dead end.

As I turned to walk away, the locks clicked and the door creaked open. A small woman stood in the doorway and glared out at me.

"Come in," she said curtly.

I hesitated.

"Or don't." She moved to close the door and I rushed back up the steps and slipped inside.

She locked and bolted the door before skirting around me. "This way."

The house itself was tall but narrow. I could have crossed from one side to the other in three strides. It was dark, despite the light outside. Every window was closed and shuttered, and while it hadn't been visible from the outside, I now saw that some of them were painted black to blot out any scrap of daylight that may have managed to seep in.

What little light there was came from a cluster of oil lamps and candles. Something dark and furry snaked through my legs and I let out a strangled yelp.

"Scared of cats?" the woman asked over her shoulder.

I struggled to see the creature in the dark and while my mind had conjured an image of some giant rat, it was indeed only a black cat. It purred softly as it rubbed its back against my leg. I scooted it away with the side of my foot and it looked at me as if I'd kicked it. It hissed and slunk off into the corner where, judging by the smell, it would probably relieve itself.

The woman led me back to a sitting area near the rear of the house. There was a table and two chairs situated in the center of the room. Against one wall stood a shelf stocked with small bottles and jars. She sat down and gestured for me to do the same.

"I'm Miss M," she said. "I don't make a habit of speaking to my clients about one another. They come to me for a reason. I don't ask questions. I don't judge. And I'm discreet about our dealings."

"Your clients?" I asked. "What is it you do, exactly?"

She grinned, showing a few missing teeth and a blackened tongue that moved behind her lips like a snake. I leaned away from her.

"I am a seller of rare things," she said. Her brows were white as snow against her fawn skin as she raised them. "Does that surprise you?"

"I don't think so," I said. "I don't know what I was expecting."

"Ah well, that's a good thing. I ask for a certain level of secrecy. Rare goods always pique the interests of the authorities, except of course when those rare items are going to the white men who run the British Museum. Funny that." She stood and went to the shelf. "As for me, I have to keep a much lower profile. Do you understand?"

"I won't tell anyone I've been here, but I have to be honest—I'm not a hundred percent certain of exactly *why* I'm here. I know Henry has been here and so has Hyde."

"People enjoy the things I have here," she said. "I have a Hand of Glory, a pair of Seven League Boots, tools for alchemy, for witchcraft."

"Witchcraft?" I asked. "Alchemy? When you said you kept rare things, I thought you meant paintings or rare books."

She cackled hoarsely. "I didn't say I practiced those things or believe in them, but there are people who do, and they pay handsomely for the things I collect."

"What did the Jekylls procure from you?" I asked. Henry and his father were ardent men of science—I couldn't imagine what either of them might need from a place like this.

"Why should I tell you?" she asked.

I took a breath and tried to decide how honest I should be with her.

"Dr. Jekyll's son Henry is very dear to me," I finally said. "He and I had been close for a very long time, and then he started to change." I shifted in my seat. "He said things I know he couldn't mean. He started to pull away from me."

"People grow and change," said the woman. "Happens all the time. I cannot count the number of people who have passed in and out of my life."

"That's not what this is," I said firmly. "He is different now. Sometimes when I look in his eyes it is as if he doesn't know me or recognize me as anything more than an acquaintance. And the part that scares me most is that it's not an act. It's not as if he's pretending to have forgotten everything we've shared. I fear he may have actually forgotten, though I cannot understand how that could be. That is the truth and it is the only reason I'm here. I don't care about your business dealings or what items you have stocked. I'll take whatever I learn here to my grave." I stared into her face and thought I saw something like pity. "Please, help me."

Miss M reached up and took from the shelf a large clay jar topped with a tightly fitted lid. She set it on the table, then sat down again.

"I do not consider myself an expert on many of the things I collect, and to be very honest, I don't always concern myself with their intended purposes," she began. "I simply pass the items along to those who pay the right amount. However, the substance Dr. Jekyll has been buying from me has become exceedingly difficult to secure. It is among the rarest of the things I keep here and so it piqued my interest."

She opened the lid and tipped the jar toward me so that I could see inside. It was full of a powdered substance ground to the consistency of flour and was a deep purple color.

"What is it?"

"It comes from a plant grown in the Pyrenees mountains. An orchid of some kind. It has been used in folk medicine for generations to induce a trancelike state when ingested."

"It's a sedative? Like laudanum?" I asked, reaching into my memory to retrieve what little I remembered from my chemistry studies.

"Not like laudanum," Miss M said. "I don't know how it works. I only know that once I was careless with the jar and managed to let a bit of it transfer to my fingers. I touched my mouth and the next thing I remember I was in the street in my night-clothes. I remember every bit of it, but I could not intervene in my own actions. It was as if I were watching myself from the outside." She laughed lightly. "It works on the mind in ways I do not understand. Turned my lips purple for a week, too."

With a shock I remembered the purple tinge on Henry's lips the night of Lanyon's party and the purple liquid in the flask. Henry was consuming it.

"And this is what is in the boxes that the Jekylls send for?" I asked.

"Yes," she said. She put the lid back on the jar and folded her arms across her chest.

There was a knock at the door.

Miss M stood. "I apologize for the interruption. Wait here." She went down the hall to answer the door, and not a moment later there was a flurry of footsteps.

"I need every last bit of it!" a man yelled.

I recognized the voice at once. I stumbled to my feet searching for a place to hide but it was too late. Dr. Jekyll barreled into the room and stopped dead in his tracks when he caught sight of me.

"Utterson," he said. The look in his eyes was like nothing I'd ever seen. It was pure, unfiltered rage, tinted with malice, and draped in despair.

Miss M entered the room and Dr. Jekyll blocked the exit with his body.

"No need to yell, Jekyll," Miss M said.

"Shut up and give me the powder," Dr. Jekyll barked. He rounded on me. "And you. You're coming with me."

"To see Henry?" I asked hotly. "Or to see Hyde? I know you've been hiding him in your laboratory."

Dr. Jekyll's brows pushed together, and he ran his hand over his bearded chin. "You have no idea what you are talking about. All of this is your fault."

I was struck silent.

Dr. Jekyll eyed the jar containing the purple powder and grabbed it, placing it inside a cloth bag. He tossed a thick envelope on the table, which Miss M picked up and then stuffed down the neck of her dress.

"Always a pleasure, Dr. Jekyll," she said, avoiding my eyes.

Henry's father grabbed me by the front of my shirt and dragged me down the hall and out the front door.

"Get off!" I snarled.

He tightened his grip as he pulled me down the alleyway in the opposite direction from which I had come. When we emerged into the street, there was a carriage and driver waiting. He threw me inside, then climbed in after me. He slammed the door shut and knocked on the wall of the cabin, sending us lurching forward.

"Where are we going?" I demanded.

Dr. Jekyll smoothed out his coat and sat back. He shook his head. "Were you aware that I have been reading your letters to my son since that first summer you spent apart from him?"

A thin film of sweat broke across my forehead. I shoved my hands between my knees and squeezed my legs together to keep from trembling. I would not allow Dr. Jekyll to intimidate me this way. In that moment, he reminded me so much of Sir Carew.

I lifted my chin and looked him in the eye. "Then you are aware of how much I care for him," I said.

"Oh yes," he said, laughing. "Indeed I am." He opened and closed his hands. "I thought that if I gave Henry a chance to see the error of his ways he would correct them on his own. I let it go on for far too long, and it became clear that he was in over his head. You have quite an effect on him."

"You act like I've cast some spell on him," I said angrily. "You've read all of our letters, so you must also know that it was Henry who approached me, and he wasn't wrong to do it."

Dr. Jekyll leaned across the narrow gap between us. His wiry salt-and-pepper beard was untrimmed, the whites of his eyes bloodshot. Even through his veil of hatred he looked exhausted. "You expect me to believe that?"

"I don't care what you believe," I said. "It is the truth."

Dr. Jekyll sat back and gazed out the window. "This ends now. But because I know how persistent you can be, I want you to hear it from Henry's own mouth. We can let this fall away from us, Utterson. You can carry on with your pathetic existence, and my son will be able to excel as much as he is allowed." He looked at me, and in his face I saw every sorrowful look my own father had ever given me. "We have so much stacked against us already. Surely you can understand."

"I understand that I cannot change who I am," I said.

Dr. Jekyll raised an eyebrow. "Oh, but you can. And I have found a way to do just that."

CHAPTER 25

DEATH IN THE LABORATORY

DR. JEKYLL PULLED ME OUT OF THE CARRIAGE IN FRONT OF HIS family's house. We stumbled up the front steps and went inside. Mr. Poole came out from the sitting room, and when he saw me in the doctor's grip, his expression went blank.

Dr. Jekyll shoved me forward and locked the door behind him.

"Henry!" he bellowed. He cocked his head to the side and glanced toward the top of the stairs. When his son didn't appear, he grabbed my arm and pulled me through the kitchen and out the back door into the garden.

"Dr. Jekyll, please!" Mr. Poole called after us. "This is unnecessary!"

Henry's father pressed forward as if he didn't hear a single word. A woman cried out somewhere behind me, but Dr. Jekyll had a hold on me in such a way that I could not turn to see who it was. We burst through the outer door to the laboratory and into the darkened hall.

"This ends now." Dr. Jekyll repeated the words as if they were some kind of incantation. As if saying it over and over again would make it true. "This ends now. This ends now. *This ends now!*"

I could barely hear over the rush of blood in my ears, over the thunderous crashing of my heart. I clawed at Dr. Jekyll's hand but he would not let go.

When we came to the inner door, it was closed, but the fractured frame gave a glimpse of the room on the other side. Someone moved across the opening, and Dr. Jekyll grasped the handle and pushed. It didn't budge. He let go of me and slammed his fists against the door.

"Henry!" he screamed. "Open the door this instant!"

He beat against the door and it opened only an inch or so before slamming into something that had been wedged against it from the other side. I leaned against the wall, my legs wobbly underneath me, as Dr. Jekyll raged.

"This ends now!" He slammed his shoulder into the door and whatever was stopping it gave way. He fell into the opening, and I pressed off the wall and vaulted over him into the laboratory.

It was eerily silent, as if I had stepped into an empty room. Dr. Jekyll groaned as he attempted to stand and immediately sank back to the floor, clutching his right knee.

I moved between the tables, which were scattered with broken glass beakers and spilled liquid. I froze, suddenly terrified to take another step.

"Henry?" I called.

A whimper sounded from the corner. Henry stood there with a glass beaker full of the strange purple liquid pressed to his lips. Before I could call out to him, he drank the tincture in one gasping gulp.

He cried out and staggered forward. His mouth gaped open, his eyes wild and terrified.

I took one tentative step forward and Henry suddenly collapsed. I rushed to him and knelt beside his too-still frame, the empty flask still clutched in his hand.

Dr. Jekyll's feral howls split the air, and Mr. Poole's hurried steps pounded the floor as he rushed in.

Miss M had described her experience with the purple mixture as akin to being outside of herself, watching as a spectator. I hadn't consumed the potion—the poison, whatever it was—but that is how I felt. I could see myself kneeling next to Henry's lifeless body, and from that vantage point I could see his brown trousers, his jacket lying open, exposing his soiled shirt—and the stain at the collar. He was wearing Hyde's clothes.

I leaned forward and put my head on his chest. When I felt nothing, no movement or heartbeat, I looped my arms around him and pulled him close to me. The first sound I heard when my senses began to wake up from the initial shock was my own wailing, mixed with Dr. Jekyll's anguished moans and Mr. Poole's frenzied pleas.

"Is he breathing?" Mr. Poole shouted.

I looked down into Henry's face. Was he? His eyelids were half closed, his lips parted. The hair at his temples was coated in some kind of white substance, and it took me a moment to realize it wasn't that at all. His hair had turned almost white.

Henry's jaw suddenly fell open and a rattling gasp escaped his throat. I almost dropped him, but got ahold of myself just in time to lower him gently to the floor.

His chest rose and fell. He didn't open his eyes or move, but he was alive.

I gently touched the side of his face and took his pulse against the ticking of Mr. Poole's pocket watch. A set of hands clamped down on my shoulders and yanked me up off the floor.

Dr. Jekyll slammed me against the wall, and pain bloomed in my shoulder.

"You've killed my son!" Dr. Jekyll screamed.

"He's not dead!" I shouted into his face.

"He might as well be!"

A woman's voice cut through the chaos. "What in god's name is happening here?"

Henry's mother stood in the doorway in her traveling coat. She marched across the room and shoved her husband back.

"Get away from him!" she said, in a way that made Dr. Jekyll immediately shrink from her.

I rushed back to Henry's side and when his mother caught sight of him, the pained expression on her face broke my heart all over again. She knelt beside him and took my hands in hers, guiding them toward Henry.

"Cradle his head," she said quietly. She tore open his shirt and pressed her ear to his bare chest. She sat back and turned to Mr. Poole. "Please assist Gabriel in moving him to my room while I call a doctor."

"*I* am a doctor!" Dr. Jekyll shouted.

Mrs. Jekyll stood, marched up to her husband, and slapped him so hard the noise split the air. "You have long ago abandoned your oath!" Disgust hung from her words like rotted flesh from bone. "Get out of my sight." She turned her back on him and helped Mr. Poole and me transfer Henry into the main house.

We placed him in his mother's bed and stripped him of his soiled clothes, replacing them with a clean dressing gown. Mrs. Jekyll sent for a physician and then joined me and Mr. Poole at Henry's bedside. Dr. Jekyll was not permitted upstairs, and I would have feared for his safety had he tried— Mrs. Jekyll set a cast-iron fire poker by the bedroom door and instructed Mr. Poole to use it on Dr. Jekyll if he attempted to enter the room.

Henry's chest rose and fell. When his breaths took too long to repeat themselves, Mrs. Jekyll noted it on a piece of paper and nudged him gently in his side, a little reminder to breathe. We said nothing for a very long time.

It was Mr. Poole who finally broke the silence. "Mrs. Jekyll, I sent a dozen letters to your mother's residence."

"Is that where he told you I was?" she asked. "He sent me to collect some items he purchased for his laboratory. He specifically said they needed to be hand carried. But when I arrived on the Isle of Mull to collect them, his contact had no idea I was coming. And then the weather—" She stopped short. "Mr. Poole," Mrs. Jekyll said, her voice wavering. "What has happened to my son?"

Mr. Poole shook his head. "I knew if you had been where Dr. Jekyll said you were, you would have responded to my letters." His eyes misted over.

I cradled my head as Mr. Poole recounted the strange series of events. A sob escaped me, and Mrs. Jekyll came around the bed and put her hand on my shoulder. At some point the doctor arrived and began to examine Henry.

He noted the strange staining on his lips; I recounted to him that I'd seen Henry drink some kind of tincture. He asked what it was and I relayed what I had learned from Miss M. The doctor administered a tonic to Henry, who was still unresponsive, and finally told his mother there was not much more he could do without knowing exactly what it was Henry ingested. He instructed Mrs. Jekyll to watch Henry closely and to call for him if his condition worsened. He then left to speak to Dr. Jekyll. Their conversation ended with Dr. Jekyll forcibly removing the man from the residence.

Mrs. Jekyll slumped into a chair next to the bed, and Mr. Poole brought her a cup of tea. She sipped it quietly and then turned to him. "Would you excuse us for a moment?"

"Of course," Mr. Poole said. He went out and closed the door behind him.

"I should have been here," she said softly, slipping her hand into Henry's. "I knew my husband was trying to keep me away, but I thought he was merely having an affair."

I glanced up at her, unsure of how to respond. "I'm sorry," I said. "I knew something was wrong. I tried to get to the bottom of it but I couldn't. I'm still not entirely sure what happened." Henry's clothes lay in a rumpled heap on the floor. "Can I tell you something?"

Mrs. Jekyll straightened up. "Of course."

"When I found Henry in the lab he was wearing those clothes." I pointed to the pile. "But I had been here just yesterday and I spoke to Hyde in the laboratory."

"Hyde?" Mrs. Jekyll asked, her face drawn tight. "He came back?"

"Mr. Poole thinks he never left. Maybe that's why Dr. Jekyll sent you away."

She gripped the blanket covering Henry's legs. "Perhaps."

I tried to think of how I could explain to her what was bothering me most. I stood and went to the pile of clothes and shook them out, laying them across the end of the bed. I wanted to be sure before I proceeded. I examined the trousers. They were light brown with a darker patch on the left knee. The jacket was dark brown and there was a small pocket on the left breast. The shirt he'd worn underneath was now torn, but the stain was visible just under the collar.

"Mrs. Jekyll, when I saw Hyde he was wearing these very same clothes."

She seemed confused. "You mean he and Henry were dressed alike?"

"No. I mean, they are the same exact clothes. I'm certain." I touched the patch on the knee and the stain on the shirt. I then moved to Henry's bedside and gently touched his temple where the hair had turned white.

I tried to recount when I'd noticed the change in Henry, and something stirred in the pit of my stomach—an ominous warning that the thoughts now knitting themselves together in my head could lead to a revelation that there would be no coming back from.

"Mrs. Jekyll," I said. "May I borrow a horse?"

"You're leaving?" she asked. "Please, don't go. Henry adores you and I know he'll want to see you when he wakes up."

I hadn't meant to sob, but I did. It broke from me uncontrollably. I wanted to believe what she said, and she knew her son better than anyone, but it was hard to accept after the way Henry had treated me.

"I'll return immediately," I assured her. "Lanyon—he left

me a letter. I haven't read it, but it has something to do with Henry."

"Why do you need a letter?" she asked gently. "Why not call on Lanyon?"

I swallowed hard. She'd only just returned. She didn't know.

"Lanyon is dead, Mrs. Jekyll," I said. The words still sounded hollow. Like they weren't to be believed.

She pressed her hand over her mouth and tears spilled down her cheeks. "How?" she whispered.

"His heart gave out," I said. "He'd been ill recently but something happened. I need to get the letter."

"Take whatever you need and hurry back," she said. She wrapped her arms around me, and I buried my face in her shoulder for a moment before leaving the room and going downstairs.

Mr. Poole met me at the first-floor landing. "Dr. Jekyll has retired to the office," he said, gesturing to a closed door down the hall. "Where are you going?"

"I need to get something I left at the boardinghouse. I assured Mrs. Jekyll I would return immediately."

Mr. Poole nodded and I left. I took the biggest horse in their stable and went to Miss Laurie's as fast as it would carry me.

CHAPTER 26

LANYON'S LETTER

MISS LAURIE LET ME IN AND FORGAVE MY RULE BREAKING YET AGAIN. I kissed her gently on the top of her head. The woman was a saint and I owed her a better explanation, but it would have to wait a little longer. I raced to my room and took Lanyon's sealed letter from beneath my mattress.

I started for the door but stopped. Whatever Lanyon had written, he'd meant for it to be read after Henry's death or disappearance. Henry lay in a state of unconsciousness, and while I feared for his well-being, I could not allow thoughts of his death to enter my mind. It was too much to bear.

I struggled with the promise I'd made to Lanyon. I wanted to honor it, but circumstances had changed. I allowed myself to believe that Lanyon would have forgiven me and opened the letter.

My Dearest Gabriel,

What I will reveal to you in these pages will be impossible to fully understand. I do not understand these events myself but I will do my best to explain them before I run out of time.

The night of the party, I was livid over Henry's treatment of you. I thought on it for days before I took a carriage and went to Henry's home. I did not want to disturb his parents or anyone else, so I waited to see if I could catch him leaving on some errand. He didn't come out of the house but another familiar face did. Hyde. I saw him go into the alleyway and I followed.

He entered the rear door of the Jekyll residence and he did not pull the door closed behind him. He was distracted, talking to himself.

I waited in the alley as he went in and then I heard Henry's voice. My anger got the better of me, my dear Gabriel. I barged in, ready to tell him exactly what I thought of him and how he'd treated you. Imagine my surprise when I found myself in Dr. Jekyll's laboratory. I was taken aback, but I tell you now that what I saw is not to be believed. I cannot fathom it, Gabriel.

What I saw will be the end of me. I know that now and so I must commit this to paper.

Hyde had his back to me. I did not see Henry. Hyde picked up a glass bottle full of a purple liquid, and as he brought the glass close to his body, his other hand shot out and stopped it. It was as if he were fighting with himself. Right hand against left.

I stopped where I was. He had not yet noticed me and I was confused. His left hand shook violently as his right pushed against it. And then he spoke . . . in Henry's voice. He said, "Go away. I don't want you here." And, Gabriel, I know you will *think me mad, but god as my witness, Hyde's voice answered from inside the very same body. It said, "We are one."*

The left hand rose and pushed the glass to his lips and he drank it. He slumped over on the table and began to moan. His white hair turned dark and his clothes suddenly seemed to fit him looser than they had before. It was then that I cried out. I could not contain it and Hyde turned to face me. His face—I don't know how—but it changed. Hyde's features melted away. His jaw narrowed. His eyes were suddenly smaller and the face that stared back at me was that of Henry.

I nearly dropped the letter and staggered back against the wall, my heart knocking against my ribs.

I felt as if my chest were crushed in a vise. I could not breathe. What I saw horrified me in a way from which I will never recover. Gabriel, something terrible has befallen Henry. I cannot say what but as I compose this, my condition worsens. The shock of it has overwhelmed me and I fear I will not live to see this through.

Hyde is Jekyll. Jekyll is Hyde. They are one and the same. A right and left hand.

How and why they have become separated I do not know, but it must have something to do with the purple liquid. I fear now that Jekyll knows I am aware of his secret, he will take drastic measures to keep it from getting out. I trust only you with this information because I know that you care for him. I wish I'd had a chance to tell you that I cared for you, too.

Perhaps this revelation is too much to share while Henry is still present. Perhaps it is best to wait until he is gone to reveal it. I do not know.

Whatever happens, I trust that you will make sense of it. You deserve so much, Gabriel. Never forget that.

Know me forever as your friend, in this life and the next.

Ever yours,

Lanyon

I had no tears left to cry. But fear . . . of that I still had plenty.

CHAPTER 27

What Is Done Cannot Be Undone

I RODE BACK TO THE JEKYLL RESIDENCE AT A GALLOP, AND STILL IT felt as if we were wading through water or sand. I didn't know what I would say to Mrs. Jekyll or even to Henry when I got there.

Henry and Hyde were one and the same. It made no sense, but I believed Lanyon because I'd seen it, too. I hadn't known what it was at the time, but Enfield and I had seen Henry's face change as we stood in the garden.

When I reached Leicester Square, I dismounted before the horse had come to a complete stop. I rushed up the steps and let myself in, not bothering to knock. I was met with angry shouting. The door to Dr. Jekyll's office stood open.

I slowly approached the door and saw the back of Mrs. Jekyll's head as she stood in front of his desk. Dr. Jekyll leaned back in his chair with his eyes closed.

"He is my son and I demand to know what role you've played in all of this!" she shouted.

"You saw how he was with Utterson," Dr. Jekyll snapped. "You saw how they looked at one another."

"I saw how happy he was," she said. "I saw him happier than he'd ever been cooped up in that lab with you!"

Dr. Jekyll slammed his hand down on the desk and I jumped. "He is brilliant and I was not going to allow him to squander his opportunities!"

"His brilliance wasn't diminished because he cared for Gabriel," she said. "You could have minded your own business! You could have been there for him regardless!"

"And be ostracized for it? Shunned in polite society?!"

"In case you hadn't noticed, that polite society thinks you're nothing but an uppity Black man who has overplayed his hand." She sighed and her shoulders rolled forward. "They hate us. They always have and still you strive to be among them. You think if you have enough money and power you can be one of them. You can't. And neither can Henry and neither can I. And why *should* we want that? Wake up, you fool!"

I stepped into the room, knowing I was out of line, that it wasn't my place, but Dr. Jekyll knew more than he was saying.

"The tonic you crafted with the purple powder split Henry in two," I said.

Dr. Jekyll slowly rose to his feet, glaring at me.

"What tonic?" Mrs. Jekyll asked in a whisper. Her entire frame shook as she rounded on Dr. Jekyll. "What did you do?"

"He has been experimenting on Henry," I said. A clear picture was beginning to unfold in my mind, and it was devastating. "He wanted to excise from Henry any feelings he had for me. But he didn't anticipate what would happen." I looked to Mrs. Jekyll. "The tonic created Hyde. He and Henry are one and the same."

"How did you—" Dr. Jekyll came around the desk and Mrs. Jekyll stepped between us. "How did you know that?"

"It's true?" Mrs. Jekyll asked.

"Don't you see what I was trying to do?" Dr. Jekyll bellowed. He stumbled back to his chair and collapsed into it. "I don't want my son to have to bear the burden of caring for you! I don't want that! I did what I could to put a stop to it, but he wouldn't listen, and so I had to take things into my own hands!" He slammed his hands on the desk again. "But in Hyde I'd created a manifestation of his love for you." He glared at me. "I had to do something to turn Henry's attention away from Hyde, to show him how truly terrible that aberration is! So that he would never want anything to do with it ever again!"

A thought bloomed in my mind and I stepped past Mrs. Jekyll.

"Carew," I said.

The look on Dr. Jekyll's face confirmed what I had begun to

suspect. He was responsible for Carew's death, and while I did not mourn the man, I had one question.

"Why?" I asked.

"To show Henry how despicable Hyde is! To show him how he would do well to rid himself of the fiend."

"You framed him for Carew's death hoping Henry would fear him?" I asked in disbelief. "Did Henry tell you what Carew did to me?"

Dr. Jekyll scoffed. "Of course he did. It was all too convenient. Hyde had the motive, the opportunity . . . the weapon."

Mrs. Jekyll gasped and took another step back. "Murderer," she whispered. "Fiend. Liar."

"Henry was questioning me!" Dr. Jekyll bellowed. "He feared *me* when it was Hyde Henry should have been fearful of! Hyde is everything he should be ashamed of, and he must be excised by any means necessary!"

"When Hyde is suppressed, Henry is not himself!" I screamed at him. "There were times when he acted as if he didn't even know me! I thought him mad but it was you all along."

"I want nothing more than to see Henry forget you ever existed," Dr. Jekyll spat.

Mrs. Jekyll pushed me behind her. "What kind of monster are you?"

"Monster?" Dr. Jekyll repeated.

He didn't see it. He couldn't see himself for what he truly was.

There came a sound from the hall. Footsteps. I waited for

Mr. Poole or Miss Sarah to walk into the office, but the steps proceeded to the kitchen. There was a click—the sound of a lock being turned and the back door creaking open.

Henry's parents were staring at each other, locked in a sort of standoff—neither of them seemed to have heard the noise. I shifted from one foot to the other and leaned out into the hall. A sinking feeling settled in my bones.

A moment later, Mr. Poole was racing down the steps. "Henry isn't in bed!" he cried.

I bolted down the hall and into the kitchen where the rear door was ajar. I ran out into the cold night air just in time to see the hem of Henry's crisp white sleeping gown disappear through the outer door of the laboratory.

Mrs. Jekyll moved to catch me by the elbow. "What's happening?"

I tripped down the rear stairs and across the garden scattered with dead leaves. Dashing inside, I knocked my knee on a chair that had been tipped over in the middle of the hallway. I kicked it out of the way. A commotion erupted from the garden behind me—Mrs. Jekyll's cries, Mr. Poole's shouting, and Dr. Jekyll's angry cursing.

This was his doing. All of it. He hadn't been trying to save Henry; he was trying to change him into something he wasn't.

I stumbled into the lab where Henry stood still as a corpse in a shaft of silvery moonlight that streamed through the skylight. His frame was skeletal beneath his sleeping gown.

"Henry," I said softly.

"Don't come any closer," he said. His voice was his own, but it was choked with a bitter sadness.

I stopped. Henry held in his hand a liter-size reagent bottle, filled to the brim with the viscous purple liquid. He trembled so violently it sloshed up and over the rim, staining his gown and dripping onto the floor.

"What are you doing?" I asked gently. "Put that down. You should be in bed resting."

The corners of Henry's mouth turned up, and his smile seemed to shift in the moonlight. It was Hyde's familiar grin paired with Henry's gentle eyes. I stilled myself.

"This ends now," Henry said, parroting his father's angry words.

"No," I said. "Listen to me—"

I was interrupted when Mr. Poole and Mrs. Jekyll barreled into the room behind me. I motioned for them to stop and be quiet. Mrs. Jekyll clamped her hand over her mouth and held fast to Mr. Poole.

"Henry," I said calmly. "Whatever your father has done, whatever it is he has convinced you of, he is wrong."

Henry's eyes filled with tears as the dimensions of the bones in his skull shifted. He gritted his teeth. "He isn't wrong. I cannot exist this way."

I stepped closer, keeping my eyes locked on his. "Why?"

"Gabriel," he said. "You know the answer to that."

Yes. I did. But I was still there, as was Henry. We hadn't disappeared simply because polite London society wished us to be invisible. If I wasn't rendered invisible for loving Henry, I'd be rendered invisible because of the color of my skin. There was nothing polite about it.

"We can exist," I said to him. "And we do. We endure because we have no other choice."

"I have a choice," he said. He held up the flask. "My father has given me a choice."

"No." I stepped forward and he moved the flask to his lips. I froze. "Your father tried to separate you from yourself."

"And he succeeded," Henry said.

I shook my head. "Do you not see how different you are? Do you not see how you've changed? And not for the better. And then there is Hyde. He—"

"You prefer Hyde to me," he said. "That much is clear."

"You are Hyde. Hyde is you. Hyde is all the things you have been made to believe you should be afraid of."

"I *am* afraid!" Henry cried. "I am afraid of myself! Of Hyde, because I know very well he is a part of me. The formula my father created suppressed him, but I've had to increase the dosage just to keep him at bay. I could not fathom my life without you, Gabriel. My father would not allow it, and I could not bear it."

My chest ached from keeping a sob bottled in my throat. Henry tipped his head up and looked at the sky through the skylight.

255

"Sometimes it didn't work and Hyde became the dominant one." He leveled his gaze at me. "I saw you through his eyes. I felt you through his touch. I envied him that he could cast aside his doubts. I envy him still." He looked at the flask. "If I drink enough of the formula, I can permanently suppress him, and I can be free of this burden."

"Burden?" I asked, a knot twisting in my throat. "Is that what loving me has been to you? A burden?"

Henry stared at me. "My father hates me for it. I owe him more than that."

Mrs. Jekyll was suddenly at my side. "No," she said to Henry. "You don't owe him this. Please, Henry. Please don't do this."

"I'm doing this for all of us," Henry said. "So that we may be free."

He lifted the flask to his lips.

I rushed forward and put my hand over his. "Henry, please." Tears streamed down his face. "Don't you see? I was drawn to Hyde because he is a part of *you*. And even then I longed for you, because Hyde is not fully himself, either. You are both missing something when you are separated." I pressed his hand down to his side but he still gripped the flask. "Do you remember when we went to the circus? Do you remember the moment we shared in the park?"

Something lit in Henry's eyes. A spark. His face shifted again and resembled Hyde, save for the color of his hair.

"Tell us," Hyde's voice said. "Let us remember who we are—together."

"The fireflies were brilliant," I said, clutching Henry's wrist. "They were so bright and the park smelled of firewood. The music, do you remember hearing it? Do you remember taking my hand and twirling me around, knowing full well I can't dance to save my life?"

The corner of Henry's mouth lifted.

"You were whole, Henry. And I loved you with my entire heart. You were enough just as you were and we are enough as we are—right here, right now."

Henry looked into my eyes. "I'm afraid."

I couldn't deny him that. There was much to fear. I knew that better than anyone, but I made up my mind in that moment that I would not let it rule me. "I understand. But I am here with you. We will face whatever lies ahead together."

Henry stared into my eyes, and finally, finally, I saw the boy I'd known, the boy I'd loved.

The flask slipped from his hand and shattered against the floor. He pulled me into his arms and pressed his lips against mine.

For the first time in months, I felt whole. Like I had been missing a part of myself as surely as Henry had been.

We were whole, and that was all that mattered.

CHAPTER 28

WHOLE AGAIN

DR. JEKYLL FLED WHEN THE AUTHORITIES WERE INFORMED, ANONY-mously, that it was he who was responsible for Sir Carew's death. The suspect Hyde was issued no formal apology because he could not be located, though a rumor spread that he was Dr. Jekyll's illegitimate son, and that perhaps the two of them had disappeared together.

Henry recovered from his ordeal, albeit with a permanent streak of hair blanched white at each temple. A reminder of what had been but, more importantly, of what was possible.

I helped Henry and Mr. Poole dismantle the laboratory piece by piece, and destroy every remnant of Dr. Jekyll's formula. We burned every notebook, every scrap of paper. We went through Dr. Jekyll's office and destroyed everything there as well, a task which Henry's mother was all too happy to assist with.

Henry and I took a long train ride out of London and into

the countryside, where we stayed with Miss Laurie's eldest sister. We needed time away, time to heal.

One morning, I nudged Henry out of his sleep and took him outside just before the sun rose.

We walked for a while through the patchwork of green quilted together by narrow groves of English oaks. The sun was just warming the horizon, and the golden glow cast all around was in stark contrast to the muck and grit of the city.

"I think I could stay here forever," Henry said.

I interlaced his fingers with mine and leaned my head on his shoulder.

"We could stay," I said. "I'm sure we could manage it."

He smiled. "We could. But you're saying you wouldn't miss the city? The smell of horse manure and boiled meat?"

We laughed and sat down in the knee-high grass as a gentle breeze swept through. "I think a part of me would miss the city but this place is so peaceful."

Henry smiled. "You want the best of both. But you have to choose, Gabriel."

I stared into his dark brown eyes. The streaks of white at his temples caught the glow of the morning sun. "I think I'll have both. I cannot appreciate the beauty of one without the other."

Henry smiled, and we watched the sun rise. Together.

AUTHOR'S NOTE

I read Robert Louis Stevenson's *Strange Case of Dr. Jekyll and Mr. Hyde* for the first time when I was in college. The discussion around the novella turned immediately to "man's true nature" and the monsters that live within us all. I, however, was much more interested in the duality of the dear doctor and what Mr. Hyde represented—a clear-cut personification of the almost hysterical homophobia of the late nineteenth century and Robert Louis Stevenson's desperate need to convey society's struggle with the negative, and often violent, perception of anyone considered "other."

I thought of what it must have been like for people living and working in London at the time and how, as is the case at this current moment in history, compounding marginalizations of one's own identity can make navigating everyday society, employment, education, the criminal justice system, and health care feel impossible. What then, might it have been like for the queer Black British people living in 1880s London?

My research for this project was not limited to reading Stevenson's work, though I have read *Jekyll and Hyde* no less than twenty times. I pored over David Olusoga's work *Black and British: A Forgotten History* to firmly establish that there is a place for Black people in the pages of Victorian era fiction, and that the establishment of Black people in Britain does not begin with the arrival of the Windrush. I cannot tell you how insidious and pervasive the myth of Black people simply not existing in certain time periods or geographical locations is.

In the pages of *My Dear Henry* you will find mention of historical figures and events, and while this is a work of fiction, I found it important to firmly anchor the tale in a reality where Black doctors, scientists, and educators existed. Their treatment was often abhorrent, and the stoning of Charles Woodson that is mentioned in this story was loosely based on the events surrounding the real-life lynching of Charles Wootton, a Black sailor, in Liverpool in June of 1919. My research was extensive, and relied heavily on the accounts of the history of Black British populations from noted scholars, historians, and academics. I am endlessly thankful for the work of David Olusoga, Professor Hakim Adi, Dr. Olivette Otele, Patrick Vernon, Kurt Barling, Dr. Caroline Bressey, and Arthur Torrington.

In a time period where being queer was criminalized and where being Black was enough to render you expendable, I was challenged to create a world in which two queer Black boys grapple with their own feelings while being at the mercy of an unforgiving society. Stevenson's original work is a cautionary tale of "the other." With *My Dear Henry*, what I have tried to do is offer a glimmer of hope at the end of a harrowing, sometimes frightening tale. Turning the story on its head allowed me to examine the role that homophobia and racism had to play in the lives of Gabriel and Henry. I could not write about queer Black boys in Victorian London without addressing these issues. I hope I have done it in a way that fosters a sense of empathy and compassion in my readers.

The sea and those who sail it are far more dangerous than the legends led them to believe . . .

This remix of *Treasure Island* moves the classic pirate adventure story to the South China Sea in 1826, starring queer girls of color—one Chinese and one Vietnamese—as they hunt down the lost treasure of a legendary pirate queen.

They will face first love, health struggles, heartbreak, and new horizons. But they will face it all together.

In a lyrical celebration of Black love and sisterhood, this remix of *Little Women* takes the iconic March family and reimagines them as a family of Black women building a home and future for themselves in the Freedpeople's Colony of Roanoke Island in 1863.

AVAILABLE FROM REMIXED CLASSICS

There seems to be no such thing as home in a war.

A ragtag band of misfits—two loyal Muslim sisters, a kind-hearted Mongolian warrior, an eccentric Andalusian scientist, a frustratingly handsome spy, and an unfortunate English chaplain abandoned behind enemy lines—gets swept up in Holy Land politics in this thrilling remix of the legend of Robin Hood.

Sometimes, lost things find their way home . . .

Catherine and Heathcliff—two lost souls, both cut off from their Indian heritage and forced to conform to society's expectations of them—find solace and possibly a future together in this masterful new take on Brontë's *Wuthering Heights*.

Thank you for reading this Feiwel & Friends book.
The friends who made

My Dear Henry:

A JEKYLL & HYDE REMIX possible are:

Jean Feiwel, Publisher

Liz Szabla, Associate Publisher

Rich Deas, Senior Creative Director

Holly West, Senior Editor

Anna Roberto, Senior Editor

Kat Brzozowski, Senior Editor

Dawn Ryan, Executive Managing Editor

Kim Waymer, Senior Production Manager

Emily Settle, Editor

Rachel Diebel, Editor

Foyinsi Adegbonmire, Associate Editor

Brittany Groves, Assistant Editor

Samira Iravani, Associate Art Director

Avia Perez, Senior Production Editor

Follow us on Facebook or visit us online at mackids.com.
Our books are friends for life.